GW01072111

THE HIDDEN HAND

THE HIDDEN HAND

Dr. Peter McCabe

VANTAGE PRESS
New York

FIRST EDITION

Copyright © 1995 by Dr. Peter McCabe

Published by Vantage Press, Inc.
516 West 34th Street, New York, New York 10001

Manufactured in the United States of America
ISBN: 0-533-11157-9

Library of Congress Catalog Card No.: 94-90248

0 9 8 7 6 5 4 3 2 1

CONTENTS

List of Figures

Acknowledgements

I should like to thank Prof. M. E. McCormick of Johns Hopkins University, Prof. William Coffey of Trinity College each for taking the trouble to read and advise on the manuscript; Edgar Deale for his wisdom and counsel, Mr. Michael Philips for producing the diagrams, and Mr. Liam O'Connor for checking the proof.

Foreword

As the knowledge of mankind increases, more questions are raised concerning both the origin of the universe and the meaning of life. It is a never-ending spiral in that knowledge begets questions, and the answers to those questions beget knowledge. The process does, at times, pose concerns for all of us. There are times when the discovery of some phenomenon is, somehow, used to "prove" or "disprove" the existence of God. In my own experience, I questioned whether a spiritual being could create a universe. Being familiar with statistical processes, however, I also realized that the creation of the universe by chance is statistically impossible. This book is directed at the examination of such quandaries by present and past philosophers and scientists.

Dr. McCabe systematically outlines the development of both scientific thought and philosophy down through the ages. He does so by developing a thought process and then, by quoting and paraphrasing the great thinkers of history in the evolution of that process. *The Hidden Hand* is not a book on religion, science, or philosophy per se. Rather, it is a book that well-relates the three. The book is written in a Jesuit style by one of the great Irish minds of our time. As such, the book should appeal to many of those concerned with this fascinating topic.

Michael E. McCormick
The Johns Hopkins University
Baltimore, Maryland

Preface

Everything in these little animals is wonderful, and highly deserving of our attention. The structure of their limbs, so regular, and well adapted to their mode of life; the care which they take of their young; the art with which they construct their cells; and their activity, industry and intelligence; all excite our admiration, and bespeak the agency of a superior power.

—C.G. Sturm, "Mode of Life and Labours of the Bees,"
in *Reflections on the Works of God, London, 1826*

C'est principalement dans les applications de l'analyse au système du monde, que se manifeste la puissance de ce merveilleux mistrument sans lequel il eût été impossible de pénétrer un mécanisme aussi compliqué dans ces effets qu'il est simple dans sa cause.

—*P.S. Laplace, Traité de Mécanique Céleste,* Tome III, Paris
1802

When Faraday first made public his remarkable discovery that a changing magnetic flux produces an e.m.f. he was asked (as anyone is asked when he discusses a new fact of nature), "What is the use of it"? All he had found was the oddity that a tiny current was produced when he moved a wire near a magnet. Of what possible "use" could that be? His answer was: "What is the use of a new born baby?

—R.P. Feynman, *Lectures on Physics,* Vol. II, Pasadena, 1964

Comet Shoemaker—Levy 9, captured and subsequently fragmented by the gravitational pull of Jupiter crashed into him in a series of collisions in the third week of July 1994 causing a necklace of enormous craters at approximately 43° south latitude on his surface.

Shall these erratic bodies one day become the means of turning the planets from their orbits, and effecting their destruction? Or, are they still deserts, without form and void, as was the earth before the Creator made it habitable and fruitful? These questions cannot be resolved by natural wisdom; and from our incapacity in this respect we may learn humility, and be convinced how very limited are the powers of the human understanding.

Men too frequently neglect this truth. Were it present to their hearts, the appearance of a comet would not raise in their minds so many vain conjectures and fruitless opinions. Some men regard comets as the precursors of Heaven's judgements; and some read in their aspect the destiny of nations and the fall of empires. Others again predict from their appearance, wars, famine and plagues; and consider them as the severest scourge of man. These superstitious people never reflect that a comet is a natural body which does not derange the order of the universe, and the return of which may be calculated with certainty; neither do they consider that this body, as well as the other planets, must have a much more important destination than that which superstition allows them. Are we to be told that the supreme Almighty Wisdom has placed these immense and magnificent luminaries in the firmament, to announce to a few poor creatures the fate which awaits them?

—C.G. Sturm, *Comets,* 1826

Each singularity, each unusual appearance by arresting our attention, tends to invite us to contemplate as well as to call forth our admiration of, the works of God.

—C.G. Sturm, 1826

Man's creation was no accident but the work of a higher intelligence that governs not only life on earth but the entire Universe.

—Fred Hoyle, Bernard Crick

The several quotations given above serve to highlight the purpose of this remarkable book in which Dr. McCabe seeks to justify that there is no conflict between the findings of modern science and belief in the existence of a supreme Being, drawing in the process on concepts as diverse as the measurement of the velocity of light and the discovery of the DNA molecule and explaining them in a form easily comprehensible to the layman.

—William Coffey
Trinity College
Dublin, July 1994

Introduction

Considering that twentieth-century science has transformed the world in the way it has, remarkably little of it seems to have gotten through to those who are not scientists, however intelligent they may be. In recent times, however, a more positive attitude to Christianity has developed, which is not widely recognised. Those Christians who think more deeply find themselves in a beleaguered position—a minority in a hostile world.

Two of the most profound advances in the history of science took place early in this century: Einstein's theory of relativity and the quantum theory. Both of these have revolutionary implications for us all; they involve time, space, and matter. But how many of us, sixty to eighty years after their inception, really understand their implication? One consequence of this widespread ignorance of science is that many people have a grossly out-of-date concept of what science really is. They still think of it as it was in the nineteenth century: materialistic, reductionistic, and deterministic, claiming absolute certainty for its conclusions, when none of these things are true of science as it is today.

Science and religion represent the two great systems of human thought; for the many on this planet, religion is regarded as the predominant force in people's lives, while science impinges only in respect of technology. Both science and religion have two faces: the intellectual and the social. The social face leaves much to be desired, while the scientific one confers luxuries such as medicine and engineering. It has also produced the atomic bomb and a host of other weapons of deadly destruction.

In the industrial world, where the impact of science is most conspicuous, there has been a sharp decline in allegiance to traditional religious institutions. Yet we live in a world that, despite appearances, is fundamentally religious. Islam remains the dominant force in Iran and Saudi Arabia, while in the industrial West, where religion is largely fragmented into a variety of pseudoscientific superstitions, the search for the deeper meaning of life continues. And why not?

The world's major religions are founded on "received wisdom and dogma." They are rooted in a turbulent history. They do not cope readily with changing times; they alter only when the need arises. They reluctantly keep step with modern thought and slowly abandon the severe philosophies of Plato and Seneca, in which the genius of man was sidetracked into cul-de-sacs and scientific speculation was to be tolerated if its function was to sharpen the wits and ignore truth.

Few would deny that institutionalised religion remains, for all its pretensions, one of the most divisive forces on earth. Whatever the good intentions of the faithful, the bloodstained history of religious conflict does not provide very much evidence of the Christian message. Both Christians and Jews today would share in the revulsion of religious conflict, with its historic involvement in torture, murder, and suppression. It is evident in Northern Ireland, where it has raged since 1969.

Religious belief has tended to become marginalised; it has become a matter of purely personal feeling—a sort of hobby for those who like churchgoing, hymn singing, or candle lighting. But is this really the way things are? It can be shown that many scientists today have become sympathetic to religious views in ways that many people find surprising.

This is not a book on religion or on proving there is or is not a God. Facts can speak for themselves. This book endeavours to consider the impact that the new physics is having on religious issues, which are frequently clouded in half-truths and superstition. It is written strictly with a view to avoiding technical or complicated terminology.

Chapter 1
The Hidden Hand

England supported a number of well-known biologists and naturalists in the nineteenth century. They became obsessed with life and its origin. God became displaced, and natural selection became the "in thing." This image persisted until the Second World War, when a sharp conflict arose between science and the concept of God. The problem to many was this: Does not the scientific worldview show that the world is a product of blind chance? It has no purpose, no value, no meaning—just material particles (whether atoms or smaller) bumping blindly into one another forever. This is in conflict with the Christian belief, which says that the world was created by a wise God for a purpose. How can these two conflicting views be held together? They cannot. What we really must ask is whether the scientific worldview does, in fact, show that there is no purpose and no God.

The views of many leading scientists today indicate that modern science suggests the opposite—that is, there is a purpose and there is a God. If this is true, why isn't it more generally known? It is accepted that some of the most popular writers today are biologists who are atheists. Their view is thought, wrongly, to be the only one amongst scientists. Dr. R. Sheldrake, in his book *The New Science of Life,* wrote:

> Most biologists take it for granted that living organisms are nothing but complex machines governed only by the known laws of

1

physics and chemistry. I myself used to share that point of view. But over a period of years I came to see that such an assumption is difficult to justify. For when so little is actually understood, there is a possibility that at least some of the phenomena of life depend on laws or factors as yet unrecognised by the physical sciences.

Dr. Richard Dawkins, lecturer in animal behaviour at Oxford, wrote *The Selfish Gene,* which was a best-seller. His book is representative of a number of scientists, mostly biologists, who believe that "we don't need God and we can't have purpose in the universe." He has recently written another book, *The Blind Watchmaker,* in which he claims that the old argument of design in the universe and the existence of God has been refuted by modern science.

Reverend William Paley (1746–1805) published an argument in the early part of the nineteenth century in which he wrote: "Suppose you find a watch lying on the ground and you examine it and you have no idea where it comes from; the very fact that it is complicated and intricate and obviously designed for a purpose is sufficient evidence that the watch was designed. It has a designer."

By the same token, Paley went on: "If you find a living body with an eye that obviously works and obviously looks as if it is designed for the purpose of seeing, you are forced to the conclusion that it must have had a designer."

For Paley, of course, the designer was God. Dawkins and others believe "we have an alternative and, in my opinion, more satisfactory explanation for the existence of things like eyes and other complicated objects that have the appearance of being designed for a purpose. That answer is Darwin's theory of 'Natural Selection.' " Dawkins's book *The Blind Watchmaker* attempts to explain Darwin's theory and, in a sense, replaces God with Darwin's theory in the worldview.

For biologists such as Richard Dawkins, then, God has been replaced by the theory of natural selection, which is a significant replacement because, whereas God must have known what He was doing and must have done it for a purpose, natural selection is, in Dawkin's phrase, a blind watchmaker. In other words, the whole universe, according to Dawkins and others, is the product of blind change: no purpose, no foresight, just a long chapter of accidents—chemical mistakes in the replication of DNA accumulating over vast periods of time.

Few biologists agree with Dawkins. Dr. Arthur Peacock, biologist and director of the Ramsey Institute, Oxford, is one of the many who strongly disagree. Peacock believes that a sufficient explanation of the world, in terms of pure chance, can be given. Insisting that one must first understand what one means by "chance," he makes the point that chance phenomena are quite well known in physics, for example, the collision of the molecules in a gas at the molecular level, while at the microscopic level the behaviour of the gas, as a whole, is orderly and complies with well-known laws. So the operation of chance at one level leads to lawlike behaviour at another. (Chance is used here to describe events that appear random and purely statistical in operation.) Alternatively, to say that something happens "by chance" is to say that we cannot assign a particular cause for it. But it is unreasonable to turn a confession of ignorance into a triumph of science; to claim we don't know the cause for something when it is purposeful begs the question.

Dr. Peacock states:

> ... it is only through chance operating at the molecular level of genetic material, for example, that all the potentiality of that material can be explored and elicited on the surface of this planet and probably on the surface of other planets unknown to us. I would say that chance is the most efficient way in which one could explore the potentialities of the given order of the universe—assuming it is made up of the stuff that we believe it to be.

3

David Bartholomew, professor of mathematical statistics at the London School of Economics, confirms the view of Peacock and goes further: "... contemporary physics believes that there is fundamental chance in sub-atomic processes. It does not rule out the existence of scientific laws—those of Newton and others. When one has the aggregate effect of very large numbers of chance events one gets purpose: one obtains order from aggregates."

It is not difficult to demonstrate mathematically that random mutation can be so ordered that the outcome is inevitable. This is demonstrated in the evolution of species, which takes place in distinct jumps from plateau to plateau over vast periods of time. There is, moreover, no evidence in the fossil record to support Darwin's theory of evolution, that is, that it takes place at a uniform rate. The theory simply became holy writ with the passage of time.

The processes involving chance and evolution still tell us nothing about life or its origin. The books tell us that life is "a mystery" and its origin is from primordial sources. *The Cambridge Encyclopedia of Life Sciences* tells us that "single cell organisms, perhaps similar to blue-green algae, were already present about 3,600 million years ago. Life must, therefore, have appeared on Earth at some time during the first 3,000 million years of the existence of the planet."

Dr. Leslie Orgel, of the Salk Institute, believes "there were very simple-cell living organisms on this planet about 3,000 to 3,500 million years ago." But there is a huge jump from single cell organisms, which he assumes emerged from primordial soup, to life. He goes on: "What we know with a fair degree of certainty is that the forms of life, present on Earth today, are derived from a single origin more than 3,000 million years ago. What we can't be certain of is were there other forms of life in those early times which died out leaving no trace?" This statement is based on guesswork.

It is clear that there was no life on the surface of the Earth at the time of its molten-mass formation. Some of the material from which life might have been fashioned eventually got there. Whence did it come? There was no oxygen. The atmosphere was very different from what it is today. Chemically it was a reducing atmosphere; iron, if exposed, would rust quickly or form a coating of iron oxide, which could react with hydrogen sulphide to form iron sulphide. Our older rocks contain abundant quantities of iron sulphide, which confirms the nature of the original atmosphere. It is believed that with the passage of time living organisms capable of photosynthesis "evolved." They absorbed carbon dioxide and liberated oxygen to the atmosphere. But how did the living organisms originate? Stanley Miller, Leslie Orgel, and others have satisfied themselves that life can emerge from a thick primordial soup, which in turn gives rise to amino acids and nucleotides. The trick, they say, "is to combine them chemically to make short pieces of protein." Replication, they claim, will follow. This, according to many scientists, is the mechanics of how life began, but it is far from the answer. It is fantastic wishful thinking. If biologists are pressed further on the matter, they are unanimous in stating that:

Life is so improbable, that it cannot possibly occur in practice. We just don't know enough about the chemistry of life. When we know a lot more about the way molecules are organized under these peculiar circumstances, then it may be possible to make some sensible statements as to how likely or otherwise the origin of life is.

There is another aspect: With the advent of the radio telescope, man has probed thousands of light-years into the cosmic deep and noted, with the assistance of the spectroscope, an abundance of "the stuff of life" out there in that cosmic deep. Formaldehyde, cyano acetylene, ammonia, water molecules, amino acids, nucleotides, etc., are all present as ready-made material in the silent deep. The solar system, with its associated planet Earth, is constantly sweeping through those vast regions filled with the "stuff of life." Is our planet being showered with it? Fred Hoyle (one of the foremost minds in astronomy today) and Robert Iastroc (NASA Godard Institute of Space Studies) have concluded that the earth has long been showered with tons of interstellar dust teeming with life organisms. For that reason they completely refute the theory that living cells first emerged by chance from a "primordial soup" from which, according to Darwin and others, "life's myriad species of plant and animal developed by natural selection with the traits necessary for survival of the fittest."

"Absurd," says Hoyle. "Man possesses properties that random selection could never produce." "How," he asks, "could the accidental coupling of chemicals in an organic ooze alone produce the 2,000 enzymes essential to life? The chances are so minute as to be 1 in $10^{40,000}$ or about the same as the chance of throwing an uninterrupted sequence of 50,000 sixes with an unbiased die."

Moreover, man developed many qualities that have nothing to do with survival: a consciousness, moral and religious impulses that frequently fly in the face of survival, as evidenced by the thousands of religious martyrs of diverse faiths who have gone to the stake rather than renounce their beliefs.

Hoyle is convinced that the origin of life lies beyond the Earth. Francis Crick (who shared the Nobel Prize for determining the DNA structure) holds the same view. Both Hoyle and Crick contend that "man's creation was no accident but the work of a higher intelligence that governs not only life on Earth but the entire universe." There are many other scientists who now hold that the origin of life is extraterrestrial. By any standard, evolution with its extraordinary ingenious and diverse ways will remain one of the wonders of the world; life *is* a mystery. Let us examine some facts.

Chapter 2
Early Progress

Science may be described as systematic formulated learning. It is concerned with devising good techniques for finding out more about how the world works. The science of physics, in particular, directs its attention toward properties of materials, laws of mechanics, and a study of the interaction of matter and energy—how things work in nature.

Man's earliest progress in science was in astronomy. From the dawn of recorded history, the Arabs and Greeks realised that there was order amongst heavenly bodies; planets and stars manifested distinct regularity in relation to their motions. Man's pursuit of knowledge from very early times brought to the fore some of the world's finest brains: Euclid, Archimedes, Copernicus, Galileo, Kepler, Descartes, Newton, and others. These men worked under the greatest difficulties in their time.

In Rome by A.D. 1600, in spite of the Reformation, the old order still obtained. Theology was still the queen of the sciences, and all branches of knowledge were subject to church control. Knowledge was politics and any break from the traditional worldview could not be tolerated without a power struggle. For that reason the career of Galileo Galilei is of importance. He was born in 1564 and lived and worked in and around Padua, Pisa, and Florence. He was a creative man; he was also somewhat arrogant. He was devout but also knew the politics under which he lived. His hero was Archimedes, engineer and mathematician.

Galileo refused to live in the world of medieval superstition; he claimed "it blinkered him and falsified the true nature of the world around." He saw the heavens as a world of ceaseless motion:

> there is in nature perhaps nothing older than motion and I've discovered some properties of it not hitherto observed.

He was of course commenting on his law of falling bodies: it was he who discovered that all bodies, irrespective of size, fall to the ground at the same rate.

It was at this stage of his life that he launched an attack on Aristotle's natural philosophy—on which the Church has always relied. Galileo showed that behind the appearance of nature there is nothing but a beautiful mathematical order. He was the first to turn a telescope on the heavens. What he saw there was not the closed Earth-centered universe of Archimedes, but that of Copernicus "with the countless stars across infinite space." Galileo was the first to see in 1610 that Jupiter had at least four satellites: "If that was so for Jupiter and her four heavenly bodies, why not the Earth also fly through space and carry with it its own satellite, the moon."

The implications for theology were immense. What Galileo saw in the universe was both new and dynamic; motion was inbuilt and perpetual: a body that is moving will continue to move until something stops it. This is one of Newton's laws, that action and reaction are equal and opposite. Momentum (velocity) is conserved; it is no longer necessary to appeal to the action of "a prime mover who keeps the universe energised from moment to moment." So Aristotle's old argument "motion to God" broke down.

It had become possible for science to explain the workings of the physical world without having to refer to theology. Science was escaping from religious control, a grip that had kept man in darkness and shadow for the previous fifteen hundred years. He had hitherto been deprived of his God-given right to look upwards, out, and on.

Galileo committed his successors to seeing a world as a machine—a wonderfully ordered machine that had nothing to do with superstition or Greek philosophy. His discoveries were easily seen as threatening, and he had to be silenced. How the Church punished him is history.

Galileo's successor, Isaac Newton, verified the mechanics governing the Earth and the heavens. He had reached the turning point in classical science. Newton wrote to Robert Hooke: "If I have seen further than Galileo or Descartes, it was by standing on the shoulders of giants." Who were these giants? In Trinity College, Cambridge, where Newton's works are to be seen, we find the works of those giants: Euclid, Descartes, Kepler, and Galileo.

It was Kepler who discovered the laws that governed the planets' motion around the sun in their respective orbits. Galileo, some thirty years earlier, had written a refreshing dialogue on mechanics. Euclid also played an important role in Newton's thinking. His elements of geometry were written in a style that Newton found "fascinating—a prototype of clear logical presentation."

From these works, Newton produced his three great laws of motion that dominated mechanics for the next three hundred years: these laws are as valid today as ever in relation to ordinary motion. In simple terms they describe the influence that forces have on bodies at rest or in uniform motion.

Newton conceived the laws in 1666 at his home in Woolsthorpe, where he worked, rather than work at Cambridge, where he would be more likely to catch the plague that ravaged England that year.

He was in many respects a strange individual: he boasted that he masticated each mouthful of his food many times more than any other man and that he never had an affair with a woman. He was not known to be homosexual. When asked why he did not explain how gravity acts; " . . . you have not explained how action at a distance could take place," he always answered in the same terms: "I do not make hypotheses; I do not deal in metaphysical speculation. I lay down a law and derive the phenomena from it."

Kepler was very different from Newton, being warm, charming, and kind. He was the first to realise that a force must exist between the Earth and the sun that keeps pulling the planet away from the straight-line path it would otherwise follow. A simple analogy: if one were to whirl a stone attached to a string in a circle, the force in the string would be towards the centre of rotation and therefore similar in action to the force of attraction (or pull) that the sun has on the Earth. In the case of the sun, it is the force of gravity that acts; in the case of the stone, it is centrifugal force.

Kepler's first law of orbital motion confirmed that planets moved in elliptical orbits (circles that have been elorgated). This gave Newton the clue to the mathematical nature of the force of gravity. He proceeded to devise a mathematical method to enable him to place the mass of the Earth at its centre. This simplified the system of forces and the distances he had to deal with. He thus came by the universal force of gravity—for which he will forever be famous. Newton had the genius to see that the force that makes the moon "fall around" the Earth is the same force that makes apples and other things fall to Earth. According to Newton's second law, an object such as a boulder takes a greater force to give it a given acceleration than the force to accelerate a small stone or an apple. He knew from Galileo's work that all objects near the surface of the Earth fall at the same rate, and that the force of gravitation on the rock must be correspondingly greater, in proportion to its mass, than the mass of the apple.

11

He reasoned as follows: if the apple is being pulled by the Earth's gravitational force (his third law of motion), then the apple ought also to be pulling on the Earth. He concluded that the forces of gravitation must depend upon the masses of both attracting objects.

What infinite satisfaction Isaac Newton must have experienced when having tested his law of gravitation, it worked both for the heavens, for the moon and other planets, and on the earth. This law is now believed to be truly universal. It applies to us, the planets, the stars, and everything else in the universe. It will be discussed in further detail later.

William Herschel (1738–1822) was probably the first astronomer to apply Newton's and Kepler's laws to locating the planet, Uranus, which he discovered in 1781. George III was so delighted with Herschel's work that he awarded him an annual grant to enable him to quit his profession as a musician and become a full-time astronomer. In 1846, U. J. Le Verrier (1811–77) by similar mathematical methods (based on Newton's laws) located the probable position and mass of Neptune. He conveyed the findings to J. G. Galle in Berlin. It only took Galle a few hours of observation to locate Neptune, the very planet whose existence Le Verrier had predicted. This discovery ranks high in the history of science—one of the many extraordinary triumphs of Newton's gravitational theory. His gravitational laws are today used in the exacting and sophisticated analysis employed by NASA and other space agencies to assist man's exploration of remote worlds of the solar system.

*   *   *

The intellectual jump from medieval times, when the Church ruled supreme and man was generally illiterate, to the mechanistic world of Newton was profound. The world was, as a result of the discoveries of Galileo, Kepler, Copernicus, and Newton, believed to be mechanistic. Indeed, Newton himself crowned it all when he declared, at the height of his power, that "the universe is like a giant clock unwinding along a rigid predetermined pathway towards its end." Many took this to mean that free will was no more, and all of us were destined to the same end.

But every age tends to throw up fresh minds and other thoughts. Newton's time was no exception. On this occasion Blaise Pascal, a brilliant philosopher and mathematician, born in France in 1623, spoke up. Pascal saw the implications of Galileo and Newton's thinking with respect to this mechanistic interpretation and showed them to be false. Pascal's inventions: the computer, the first public transport, and the altimeter, together with a thesis on geometry, had earned him an enormous reputation. He became one of the most sought after personalities in Paris in his time. He died a young man, but not without leaving much food for thought.

Pascal had met the philosopher Descartes at one of the many intellectual gatherings of the day in Paris. Descartes had become the leading exponent of the new mechanistic science and was an uncompromising rationalist. He proved God's existence by abstract arguments and then used God to certify the validity of human reason and the existence of a mechanical universe. He claimed that after that science took over. Pascal considered such lip-service to religion abhorrent:

I cannot forgive Descartes. His whole philosophy would like to do without God, but he couldn't without allowing him a flick of the finger to set the world in motion. He had then no more use for God.

Pascal was later to write his world-famous "Pensées sur la religion," which embraced genius, science, faith, and reason:

"The whole visible world is only an imperceptible dot in nature's ample bosom. No idea comes near it . . . "

13

"To offer man an astounding prodigy, let him look into the tiniest thing. Let a mite show him its minute body incomparably more minute parts—legs with joints, veins in its legs, blood in its veins, cells in the blood, vapours in the drops. Let him divide these things still further till he has exhausted his powers of imagination.''

"Our own human body is now a colossus compared to the nothingness beyond our reach.''

"Of the two infinities of science that of greatness is much more obvious.''

"Eternal silence of these infinite spaces fills me with dread. When I survey the whole universe in its dumbness, and man left to himself with no light as though lost in this corner of the universe without knowing who put him there, what he has come to do, what will become of him when he dies, incapable of knowing—I'm moved to terror.''

"Man is only a reed, but he is a thinking reed. There is no need for the universe to take up arms to crush him. A vapour, a drop of water is enough to kill him.''

"But even if the universe were to crush him, man would still be nobler than his slayer because he knows that he is dying, the universe knows nothing of this.''

"Let us consider the point and say either God exists or he does not exist. But which of the alternatives should we choose? Reason can determine nothing. A coin is being spun at the extreme point of this infinite distance which will turn up heads or tails. What is your bet?''

"It is the heart that perceives God not the reason. The heart has its reasons of which the reason knows nothing.''

The year 1600 was a watershed. Ignorance, religious super-stition, and clerical tyranny were declining, and scientific learning was in the ascent. During the Middle Ages the language of faith shaped the essence of the world as then perceived; religion was public property and was objective. Faith and knowledge were, in fact, held as one. They began to fall apart with the arrival of classical physics. The thinkers of the day began to see the world as mechanistic, as Newton had believed. But Pascal insisted that while knowledge of the world should in the future be expressed in numbers and specific laws, that did not mean that the world had been reduced to a gigantic clock. On the contrary, he claimed that everything in nature pointed towards an holistic rather than a mechanistic system.

Chapter 3
The New Physics

In ancient times, the Greeks realised that the building blocks of matter were made up of tiny pieces held together by something. By the beginning of the nineteenth century scientists accepted the idea that chemical elements consisted of atoms; they knew nothing about the atoms themselves. The discovery of the electron by J. J. Thomson at the end of the nineteenth century and later the realisation that all atoms contained electrons provided the first important insight into atomic structure.

From the end of the nineteenth century, a host of brilliant scientists attacked the problem to determine the nature of the building blocks. In 1889, J. J. Thomson showed that atoms were uniform pieces of positively charged matter in which electrons were embedded—a sort of plum-pudding effect. But in 1911 Ernest Rutherford and his co-workers Geiger and Marsden decided that in order to find out what was inside the "plum pudding" one had to plunge a finger into it. They used alpha particles as that finger. (Alpha particles are helium atoms stripped of their orbiting electrons.) This work led to much more in the succeeding decades.

It now realized that the atom is comprised of a central nucleus around which electrons orbit at various distances from the nucleus, dependent on the nature of the element.

By the early twentieth century, the leading physicists Albert Einstein and Niels Bohr (both of whom had pioneered celebrated work on the atom and on relativity) accepted the new concepts that the atomic world was, in fact, fuzzy and nebulous, full of mystery and uncertainty—a fundamental ingredient of the subatomic. The mystery deepened as probing became more sophisticated. Prior to this, it had been customary for physicists to compare the structure of the atom, such as carbon for example, to that of the solar system; the analogy being that the sun represented the nucleus and the planets represented the electrons. This analogy quickly wore thin when it was realised that the laws governing the atomic world entirely differed from those that had hitherto been taken for granted. Classical, or Newtonian, physics was rapidly giving way to the new physics, of which the central pillars are the relativity theory and the quantum theory.

Let us now return to the beginning of the twentieth century to see the emergence of another phenomenon, that of wave-particle duality.

In 1900 Max Planck, a German theoretical physicist, was puzzled by the characteristics of radiation that he found were emitted by solid bodies. The radiation did not fit the electromagnetic pattern that the English scientist James Clerk Maxwell had established some years earlier. Einstein put Planck's mind at rest in 1905 when he showed that there was, in fact, a discrepancy in Clerk Maxwell's theory: Einstein declared that all bodies radiate energy at all times but at different wavelengths, depending on the temperature. Einstein confirmed that Planck was correct in his discovery that radiation occurs in bursts, or quanta, and not in continuous waves. Einstein's findings proved correct. His proposals immediately explained away a number of anomalies in physics, such as the photoelectric effect and others.

Einstein went further and proposed that light propagates as a series of packets of energy (called photons). This upset certain aspects of Maxwell's classical theory, which proposed that light travelled in waves. Thus began one of the great paradoxes of modern physics. It was the beginning of quantum mechanics, developed later by Edwin Schrödinger and Werner Heisenberg.

*   *   *

One of the aims of science has been to provide an exact picture of the material world around us. Physics in the twentieth century has shown that such an aim is unattainable. Special relativity has shown that there is no universal time. It gradually dawned on physicists that the universal ingredients of matter are governed by unique laws in which the observer and the observed had each a particular role to play in any scientific experiment or measurement. We will return to this matter later.

Energy—Particles and Waves

In our everyday experience there is nothing mysterious or ambiguous about the physical concept of particles and waves. They are the two ways in which energy can be conveyed from one place to another.

If one throws a stone at a window or at a person, the window will probably break, or the person will be injured. The stone has conveyed energy from the thrower to the window or the person. When one drops a stone into a lake, ripples spread out in all directions from the point of impact of the stone. It is only the motion of the water surface that is travelling from one point to another, and it is doing so in the form of waves.

It is therefore natural to ask, when one sees energy on the move, if it is being transported in the form of particles or waves. For example, the light from the sun; is it in the form of waves or particles? Or, think about the electron beam from the TV tube, carrying energy from the back of the tube to the front face. Is this energy waves or particles?

Clearly some kind of test is needed in which particles and waves behave in different ways. Hosts of tests were set up in laboratories to check the nature of waves and particles. One of the most convenient tests in this connection is to direct a beam of radiation through a couple of slits in a barrier. What appears on the screen on the other side can then be examined. Particles, fired through slits in this way, provide distinct interference patterns. (Figure 1.)

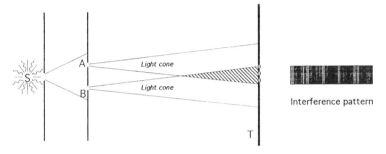

Figure 1. *Thomas Young's twin-slit experiment, interference pattern shown on right.* The light from S illuminates the two slits A and B. The light diverging from A has exactly the same frequency as the light diverging from B. It is also in phase with it. The diverging light from A and B acts as two close coherent sources. Interference thus takes place in the *shaded* region where the light beams overlap. The effect is alternate dark and bright bands on screen T, confirming that the light travels in waves.

Likewise one can study the behaviour of water surface waves in a ripple tank by allowing the parallel waves to pass through appropriate openings in a barrier in the tank. In this case interference patterns are obtained as the waves, having passed through the opening, spread out. We know from the interference patterns that they are waves.

Such tests can be applied to light using very narrow slits and a laser beam. The result is an interference pattern, signifying the wave nature of light. Only a fool could believe otherwise. But there was such a fool: his name was Albert Einstein. He showed conclusively by means of the photoelectric effect that light takes the form of particles. He also showed that light of different colours behaves like particles with different energy. For red light the energy is small; for ultraviolet light it is high. So Einstein's calculation, carried out in 1905, was wholly contradictory of the wave theory of light. However, physicists gradually and reluctantly came to accept it. He was awarded the Nobel Prize in 1922 for this work.

So our understanding of the most universal of all phenomena, light, is a little confusing. The double-slit experiment showed light to consist of waves, and the photoelectric experiment conclusively showed that light propagates as particles. There could be nothing more different than waves and particles. So it became clear that light possessed a wave-particle duality and, furthermore, that the wave theory of light and the quantum theory of light complement each other. What an extraordinary discovery!

Chapter 4
Light

The nature of scientific knowledge and truth has become the subject of serious debate. But hasn't the nature of truth taxed the minds of philosophers, scientists, and theologians ever since man could think? Yet it was a Danish philosopher, Soren Kierkegaard, at the begining of the nineteenth century, who produced the strangest answer in relation to the paradox. A wave of intellectualism, passing over Northern Europe at that time, happened to threaten Christianity. It concerned itself with whether Jesus was fully God and at the same time fully man. Kierkegaard came to the rescue: "One should not try to rationalise such paradoxes away. One should embrace them and learn to live with them as indications of the limitations of human reasoning. One should aim for a more subjective form of truth. The thinker who is devoid of paradox is like the lover devoid of passion."

Kierkegaard also said of the apparent contradiction of paradox: "When subjectivity in business is the truth, the truth, objectively defined, becomes a paradox; and the fact that the truth is objectively a paradox shows, in its turn, that subjectivity is the truth."

The wave-particle paradox, like that of Jesus being both God and man, points to there being a need for a more subjective kind of truth. Niels Bohr saw a deeper meaning in Kierkegaard's philosophy. Einstein equally subscribed to it.

Subjectivity and objectivity had taken on new meanings in physics, as had the word *uncertainty*. The atomic world in the twentieth century emerged with relativity and quantum theory proving to be amazingly successful in explaining what Newtonian physics failed to do. The old order of classical physics yielded place to the new in the space of sixty years.

$$*\qquad*\qquad*$$

When the universe was formed, its first and most common ingredient was light. What do we know about light, apart from its wave-particle duality discussed earlier?

One of the problems that arose during Newton's lifetime was the question of whether the speed of light was infinite. Its speed had to be measured somehow; it was done.

A convenient method of measuring the speed of light, in the past, was how long it took one of Jupiter's satellites to revolve about its parent planet, that is, the interval between successive eclipses. The Danish astronomer Olaus Roemer was doing just that in 1675 when he discovered that the period of a satellite of Jupiter's was longer when the Earth was moving away from the planet than some months later when the Earth was moving towards Jupiter.

Roemer calculated, correctly, that it takes light about sixteen minutes to cross the orbit of the Earth, that is, light travels at a speed about ten thousand times the speed of the Earth in orbit. He was now satisfied that light had a definite velocity.

But the speed of light can also be measured by timing its passage over very accurately measured distances on the earth. Galileo, in his time, suggested ways in which this might be done but realised that light travelled far too fast to measure its velocity using the crude techniques available to him. By far the most famous experiment was done in 1926 by the first American scientist to win the Nobel Prize, Albert A. Michelson. Velocity is defined as the distance something moves in a given time, so to measure the speed of light Michelson had to have not only a very accurate timing mechanism, but also a very accurately measured distance. He selected two mountain peaks in the San Gabriel range in Southern California; one was Mount Wilson (of observatory fame), and the other Mount San Antonio, twenty-two miles away. He needed to know the distance between two mountain peaks to a precision of only seven inches. He did it with the help of the U.S. Navy. Measurements of the distance took over a year to complete.

Michelson then used light from an arc lamp located on Mount Wilson and bounced it off a rotating eight-sided mirror nearby and then by a series of reflections to San Antonio, twenty-two miles away. From there a second series of mirrors sent the beam back to Mount Wilson, where it was redirected onto the eight-sided mirror, but this time to the side symmetrically opposite to that of the first reflection. During the light's return trip the rotating mirror had turned slightly, and the final reflected beam was passed into the viewing telescope and observed when the mirror made exactly one-eighth of a turn. It was now an easy matter to calculate how long it took the mirror to make one-eighth of a turn—the time required for the light to make the forty-four miles round-trip. (Figure 2.)

Figure 2 shows the features of Michelson's apparatus: X is an equiangular octagonal prism that can rotate at constant speed about a vertical axis. The faces of the prism are polished. When light is allowed to pass through a slit (O) from a bright source, it is reflected at A to a mirror, B. It is then reflected from plane mirror C, located at the focus of a large concave mirror, HD (Mount Palomar). The light then travels to another concave mirror, GE, on San Antonio, twenty-two miles distant from HD, and is reflected to a plane mirror, F, at focus of GE. The light is reflected back to H and thence to the focus L and on to M. From here it is reflected to the prism face N opposite to face A. The final image obtained is viewed through T.

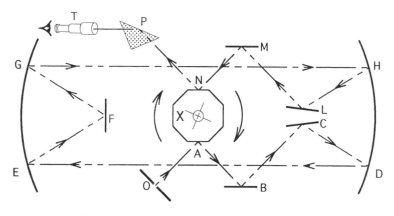

Figure 2. Michelson's rotating prism method.

When the prism is rotated to high speed the image disappears, at first, as the light reflected from it arrives at the opposite face, N, to find this surface is no longer parallel to the original surface, A, when the light took off, as it has moved. When the speed of revolution of the prism is fast enough the light reflected from A arrives at the opposite face, N, in the time taken for the prism to rotate through forty-five degrees or one-eighth of a revolution.

The experiment gave a very accurate value for the speed of light. Modern techniques for measuring the speed of light in a vacuum give a value of 299,792.458 kilometers per second. In air, the speed of light is reduced by about 70 kilometers per second. This physical constant is now universally denoted by the letter *c,* the speed of light in a vacuum. Michelson later sent light down a vacuum to measure its velocity; today matter is also sent down a vacuum tube and its velocity boosted by electrical forces to study its behaviour at very high speeds.

A few hundred miles north of Mount Wilson, in Northern California, is the Stanford linear accelerator, called SLACK. It is a two-mile-long vacuum chamber designed to test the behaviour of particles of matter under extreme velocities—it is an attempt to understand how nature works at its most fundamental level. At SLACK the lightest elementary particles—electrons—are accelerated to extremely high velocity and sent down the vacuum chamber. At first they are accelerated by impulses of 70,000 volts. Initially the electrons comply with Newton's laws of motions, since they are travelling at a speed less than the speed of the Earth or the other planets. However, an electron is so light that by the time it escapes the influence of the 70,000-volt impulse, it is travelling at half the speed of light. The procedure makes it possible to test Newton's laws of motion far more accurately than anything in the solar system.

As the electrons increase in speed they are given a further impulse (400,000 volts), which, according to Newton's laws of motion, should increase their speed to five times the speed of light. But that is not what happened: as electrons are pushed further and further, they refuse to reach the speed of light. They allow themselves to reach a speed of one-third of one percent below the speed of light, that is, 99.66 percent of the speed of light but no more. It was noted that something strange occurs to the particles as they close up on the speed of light: they increase in mass to an extent that is in the order of four hundred times their original mass. Why? They don't increase in size; they just get heavier and heavier and in doing so become more obstinate.

These tests were repeated over and over again in many countries, using a variety of types of matter. The results were all similar. The impulses given to the particles were such as to expect the speed of the particles to exceed the speed of light by three hundred times, but nothing doing.

The one-third percentage gap is gradually reduced, but it is never closed. Under such extreme conditions, Newton's laws break down and new laws are needed. These laws, whatever they are, must be similar to Newton's laws at low speeds, but totally different at high speeds.

*   *   *

From the age of fifteen Albert Einstein thought thoughts that nobody before him had ever thought. He asked questions that no one had ever asked: transparently innocent questions that turned out to have catastrophic answers—answers to problems that no one else recognised were problems.

One of his most innocent and most beautiful concepts was: ''What would the world look like if I were to ride on a beam of light?'' This question occurred to him one day when riding on a tram and looking up at the town hall clock at Berne when it read twelve noon. He reasoned thus: *If light travels at a speed of 186,000 miles per second and if I sat on a beam of light and traveled 186,000 miles away from the clock, it would take me one second. But the time on the clock, as I would see it, would still read noon, because it takes the beam of light, from the clock, exactly as long as it has taken me to travel 186,000 miles. So far as the universe on the beam of light is concerned, keeping up with the speed of light cuts me off from the passage of time.* Time stops when on a light beam! (See appendix 1.)

What an extraordinary paradox! What an extraordinary situation, but nevertheless, it has since been shown to be true. Einstein's summary of events was as follows:

Should I ride on a beam of light, time would suddenly come to an end for me. That must also mean that as I approach the speed of light in a tram or whatever, I am more and more departing from the norms around me. Such a paradox makes two things clear: firstly, there is no universal time and secondly, experience runs very differently for the traveller and the stay-at-home. My experiences within the tram, or rocket, are consistent: I would find the same laws, the same relations between time, distance, speed, mass and force as every other observer. But the actual *values* I get for time, distance, etc. would not be the same as those recorded by the man at home. In other words my clock, when travelling at high velocity, runs slower than an exactly similar clock at rest.

This is the essence of the principle of relativity, the consequences of which are enormous. One question must arise: What holds time and space and matter together for the astronaut and for the stay-at-home? It is, of course, the passage of light. Light is the carrier of information that binds us: when we exchange light signals we discover that information passes between us always at the same speed. We always get the same value for the speed of light. But time and space and mass are different for each of us, because each has to yield to the same laws, whether they be for astronaut or the stay-at-home. The speed of light has the same value for all.

Chapter 5
Stars

Astronomy became a big science in the twentieth century, but not as big as high-energy physics in the exploration of the micro-universe. Any description of the universe requires us to explain why nature mass-produces high-energy particles that continuously rain on the earth from without. Researchers learned ways of collecting and using some of these particles. Occasionally the material gathered possessed energies far surpassing what could be produced in the laboratory. Nations vie with nations and governments with governments to finance research into how this universe is constructed. The most elaborate instruments devised by man are being built. Giant particle accelerators are being developed.

The Fermi National Acceleration Laboratory at Batavia, near Chicago, which sprawls across the Illinois countryside, accelerates protons (nuclei of hydrogen atoms) to six times the energy achieved at Serpukhov in Russia, which itself has a capacity of 76,000 million electron volts (MeV). High-energy physicists have got down to business and are discovering things, fast. Whence comes this bountiful source of energy?

We know that there are many millions of stars in our galaxy (the Milky Way) and that there are millions of galaxies in the universe. Modern telescopes have taken us a little way to seeing many of the strange objects deep in space, a place that is dark and amazingly silent. To see into this darkness we require a new type of telescope sensitive to X-rays, but it must be placed in orbit outside the Earth's atmosphere to pick up X-ray photons. Such instruments have been built since the 1970s. They are, in essence, satellite observatories that examine not only starlight, but X-rays. They look out into the unknown and hitherto invisible universe and make darkness visible. Knowledge of the X-ray universe has opened up another extraordinary world.

The first studies using this technique were carried out on the Crab nebula in the constellation of Taurus, which is the debris of a star that exploded in the year 1054. Nevertheless, substantial X-ray radiation is emitted from this nebula. Its radiation is regularly photographed by satellite observatories and the data returned to Earth. Scientists at the Goddard Institute of Space Studies near Washington, D.C., can complete X-ray images of the Crab in eight or ten minutes with modern computer printouts. When this was first achieved it was discovered that the nebula was dominated by a neutron star near its centre. But before discussing neutron stars, let us consider stars generally. What are these tiny beacons of light that makes themselves visible in the night sky and sprinkle our celestial dome?

Stars are formed from clouds of dust and gas, also called nebulae, that make up a large portion of the material in galaxies. Galaxies, in turn, consist of a large collection of stars occupying a region of space well separated from other large collections of stars.

When the dust of nebulae becomes sufficiently dense, the nebulae become ''critical'' under the influence of shock waves and gravity. The dust condenses into clouds, which are dark and cold to begin with. As they condense they heat up to enormous temperatures and pressures and then begin to radiate light. They obtain their energy by the conversion of hydrogen (of which the universe abounds) into other elements. Hydrogen is first converted to helium, then carbon, and on up through the periodic table to uranium and plutonium. It was only in the 1940s and

1950s, through the work of Hans Bethe and Fred Hoyle, that the thermonuclear conversion of hydrogen to heavier elements was seen to correspond to the successive stages in the evolution of stars. Stars such as red giants, for example, are those whose hydrogen fuel has been exhausted, having been converted to helium. (This matter will be discussed further in chapter 18.)

Stars, like our sun, are therefore like gigantic hydrogen bombs that explode in slow motion. They have a life span ranging from a few million years (in the case of Deneb) to thousands of millions of years (in the case of our sun). When their fuel is exhausted they contract or explode with enormous violence, sending their ingredients, built up within their cores, hurtling through space to rain on other celestial bodies, including our Earth. This is the origin of the minerals and other elements found in our rocks and surface layers of earth—also the origin of the precious minerals essential to animal life: magnesium, sodium, potassium, chlorine, sulphur, iron, copper, manganese, cobalt, zinc, and fluorine. While some of these are required as trace elements in the body, all of them are essential to healthy functioning.

We know that there are different kinds of stars that vary in size, power, and brightness. Some are much hotter than others; the colour of a star depends upon its temperature. White stars may have a surface temperature of about fifty thousand degrees centigrade; cool red stars may be as low as three thousand degrees. The sun at six thousand degrees at the surface is yellowish. The cores of stars have temperatures of the order of 15 million degrees centigrade.

There are also variable stars, double or binary stars. Some are unpredictable and violent. Every few years a new star, visible to the naked eye, increases in brightness overnight. This is a nova, a member of a close binary system that blasts off huge quantities of material. A nova can increase in brightness by 10,000 times in a few days.

Supernovae are more rare. They result from the self-destruction of massive stars that rival an entire galaxy in brightness. The last supernova observed in our galaxy occurred in the year 1604; the one of 1572 could be seen in broad daylight, while the 1054 supernova left the wreckage known as the Crab nebula. All supernovae shatter themselves to pieces in explosions that reduce them to neutron stars—the end of a supernova. Neutron stars, predominantly composed of neutrons, have a radius of about ten kilometres, although their mass equals that of our sun. To give us a sense of scale, a piece of their matter the size of a lump of sugar would contain 100 million tons of neutrons.

Let us return to high-energy radiation and X-ray pictures. What is an X-ray picture? X-rays were discovered in 1895 by Wilhelm Röntgen. Radiation took the form of a mysterious emission from his cathode tube. He noted that the radiation penetrated flesh and cast a shadow on bones. The rays were to him a mystery, so he called them X-rays. It was later realised that X-rays were simply a very energetic version of light—electromagnetic radiation of energy high enough to penetrate the flesh. Electromagnetic radiation, for convenience, can be compared to the notes of the keyboard of a piano where the bass register corresponds to radio or infrared waves and the treble register to X-ray or ultraviolet radiation. The middle register of the keyboard may be compared to visible light.

How are X-rays produced? If electrons are shot from an electron gun in an X-ray tube so as to hit a metal target, X-rays emerge from the point of collision in the form of a stream of energetic particles. These are X-ray photons. It is these bulletlike particles, emitted from the sun and other stars, that are captured by satellite laboratories and converted into pictures in the way a TV camera does.

Our nearest star, the sun, not only emits bulletlike visible photons of light, ranging in energy from red to violet, but it also shoots out other bulletlike photons, which range from low-energy infrared to high-energy ultraviolet or X-rays. The sun is in a continuous state of activity, giving rise to huge eruptions at its surface.

In 1964 scientists at the U.S. Naval Research Laboratory (NRL) suspected that interference with radio communication might be caused by X-rays from the sun. In 1948 evidence of solar X-ray emission was confirmed.

Knowledge increased rapidly with improved launching methods of instrument-carrying rockets. A few years later a telescope was put on board Sky-lab, which took detailed pictures of the sun and noted that X-rays were continuously formed above its surface where temperatures were high enough for the generation of X-rays.

In June 1962 Dr. Ricardo Jacconi developed a powerful X-ray detector that, when placed in orbit, located an X-ray star one thousand times brighter than our X-ray sun. It was in the constellation of Scorpio. Since then hundreds of other X-ray stars have been located and plotted.

Notwithstanding, the Crab nebula is a curious astronomical object—a remnant of a star that exploded long ago as a supernova. Powerful X-ray telescopes have since located a neutron star within the debris of the Crab that is actively emitting vast quantities of X-rays.

How do neutron stars form? At a late stage in the long life of a star it swells to become a red giant, due to the battle between atomic radiation pushing out and gravity pulling into the centre. When the star's nuclear fuel is exhausted and pushing out gives up, the star shrinks to a white dwarf, shedding energy as it reduces in size. The process results in stars, originally the size of the sun, reducing to the size of our Earth or much smaller. At that stage the star consists almost entirely of atomic nuclei. It is then a neutron star of immense density and spinning rapidly due to reduction in size.

In 1970 *Ohurru,* a spinning, tilting satellite developed by Dr. Ricardo Jacconi, was launched from Kenya. *Ohurru* added a host of new X-ray stars to the celestial map—many different kinds. It was a milestone in X-ray astronomy and led to the discovery of X-ray binary stars.

It is now clear to astronomers and physicists alike how a binary system, containing two stars in close association, generates X-rays. One star is so dense (the neutron star) that it pulls its huge companion out of shape and attracts enormous quantities of heated matter onto itself, emitting X-rays in the process—just another proof of the existence of neutron stars. Binary systems show slight time lags in the reception of X-ray radiation. This enables the size of their orbits to be measured.

Moreover, in the giant cluster of galaxies in the Hercules constellation there are binary X-ray stars pulsating as rapidly as many pulses per second. There are others that pulsate at much faster rates. In the Cygnus constellation a very much more powerful X-ray source has been located. The indication is that this was the first discovery of the extraordinary phenomenon called a black hole, from which no light, no matter, and no X-rays escape. Matter is continuously spiralling into black holes, to be radiated as vast quantities of energy—another extraordinary system, a density vacuum of enormous power.

Chapter 6
Animals and Plants

Animals and plants require food to survive. They convert food to energy and use portions of it to maintain themselves. They store the remainder until the need arises. The energy is then recovered from the food by oxidation (adding oxygen), a process that involves a number of chemical steps. (Details of the process can be obtained from any standard textbook in biochemistry.) Plants are no exception to the oxidation process; they differ only in that they first make the food, using sunlight to do so, and then oxidise it. The animal kingdom feeds on what is left over.

Most people are aware that green plants and some bacteria use the energy of sunlight to manufacture sugars and other foodstuffs. This is the most important single process in the whole range of vital activities—upon it depend almost all other forms of life on Earth.

Let us briefly look at the physiology of animals and plants to get an idea of their mode of operation; animals and plants are made up of thousands of millions of cells, each of which is a tiny powerhouse and chemical laboratory in its own right (figures 3a and 3b).

We learn with astonishment, from an introduction to natural history, of the enormous variety of animals and plants that exist on this planet: forty thousand species of fungi, more than half a million species of insects, and so on. When the surprise has worn off in relation to nature's prodigality, we are then confronted with

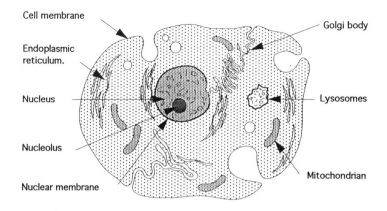

Figure 3a. Structural components of a "typical cell."

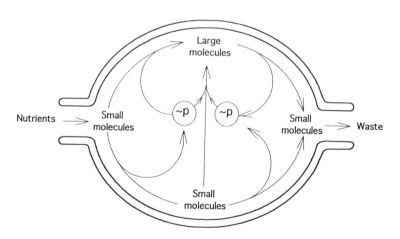

Figure 3b. Idealised cell in steady state.

her tightfistedness in relation to her chemical machinery: if the orders and divisions embracing the animal and plant kingdom were all to have their own peculiar ways of carrying on life, if chemical variations were to be matched by variations in form and structure, the task of biochemistry would be alarming. It so happens that living things exist in a variety of shapes and sizes, but the scope of their chemistry is very restricted. An example will serve to show how much there is in common between creatures widely separated on the evolutionary scale.

Yeast, for example, is a unicellular organism that breaks down glucose, via pyruvic acid, to alcohol. Human muscle also converts glucose to pyruvic acid, from which is formed the lactic acid that appears in the blood during exercise. The transformation of glucose to pyruvic acid by yeast takes place in eight stages, eight separate reactions that can be followed in the test tube. Exactly the same eight reactions take place in human muscles and in the same order. Nature insists on being tightfisted!

These are strange factors when we reflect on the ages that have elapsed since the forerunners of man and the yeast cell parted company many millions of years ago. Nature does not find it necessary to alter her methods or the machinery she uses. She does so with respect to shapes and forms—as though she has fun in doing so.

*   *   *

Before looking further into the makeup of the animal structure, let us summarise: all organisms consist of millions of cells, each containing the ingredients to differentiate and specialise to form tissue such as bone, muscle, brain, skin, blood, leaves, petals, stems, roots, etc. In the embryo these tissues grow; they eventually develop into fully blown organs before birth. The process that governs the development of animal organs and directs their shape and function is another of these ingenious and complex operations. In the case of plant life the specialised cells give rise to plant organs such as leaves, petals, barks, roots, etc.

Babies are born with organs sufficiently well developed to maintain life in the environment into which they are suddenly thrust. The choice of organs provided by nature to carry out the vital function is interesting. The manner in which they are integrated is ingenious.

Fish have developed a system to suit their environment. Land-based animals went further; they have developed to a higher degree:

1. The heart and circulatory system are designed to distribute food via the blood to the cells and remove waste products.
2. The respiratory system consists of lungs equipped with tiny capillaries and air sacs where gas exchange takes place between air and blood. The haemoglobin in blood captures the oxygen and releases CO_2 waste.
3. In the digestive system, food is chopped up in the mouth and broken down by enzymes. It is later absorbed into the bloodstream and passed to the liver and the tissues. The unabsorbed food, together with bacteria and cells shed from the lining of the intestines, is passed to waste.
4. The kidneys collect the waste products of cells (other than carbon dioxide) and excrete them after temporary storage. This waste is discharged as urine.
5. The liver is the chemical factory of the body and has many functions. It is concerned with blood, with the formation and destruction of red blood cells. It stores sugars for conversion to nonsugars such as proteins and fats. It assists in removing poison and surplus amino acids, with the resulting production of ammonia. It is the

only organ that can convert ammonia into urea. Bile fats, produced in the liver, are essential for the digestion and absorption of fat.

6. The nervous system comprises the central communication system of the body. It consists of a central part, the brain and the spinal cord. Peripheral branches serve the limbs. The system is complex, as it is the transmitter and receiver of messages from one part of the body to another. It is responsible for guidance, balance, control, and coordination.

7. Apart from its normal physiological function, the brain is probably the most extraordinary machine ever dreamed of. Scientific studies in the United States and elsewhere in the last decade show that we begin life with a bio-potential brain that, in its very early stage of development, is neither male nor female. Its sex is quickly determined by the presence or absence of the hormone testosterone. The human brain is much more dependent on environmental influences than the other species: for example, if one rears a male in the style of a female, his behaviour will become female, and vice versa. The brain regulates reproduction in adult animals. Not only does it control breeding cycles, courtship, and mating, but it also controls maternal behaviour. The thalamus and pituitary glands make the hormones that cause ovulation, milk production, and so on. It is the origin of thought, recall, creativity, emotion, and passion. Its method of achieving these is known to be extremely complex.

In addition to the seven organs mentioned above, there is a group of endocrine glands that contain various hormones, which may be proteins, steroids, or simple organic substances that are carried to all parts of the body and act as chemical messengers.

Our thoughts, actions, and perceptions are being constantly modified by the brain because of its previous experience. This means that somewhere within brain cells, fibres, synapse connections (the equivalent of one-way valves), and the chemical transmission systems are being reorganised at all times. It is known that the brain is a computer whose components are being continuously repaired, reconnected, and reprogrammed as the machine itself is working.

Chapter 7
Cosmic Forces

One of the matters to emerge from physics in the twentieth century was the fact that everything is fashioned and governed by the action of four forces on the fundamental particles of all matter. (See table A, appendix 2.)

The understanding of how the universe works is reduced to recognising those forces. There may be others.

Most of us know what electricity is—it is often described as a flow of electrons along a conductor. People are reasonably familiar with magnetism, which has the property of attracting iron filings or upsetting compass needles. Clerk Maxwell, in 1864, realised that both these forces are one and the same force under a different guise—the electromagnetic field. It covers a broad frequency band, extending from the shortest wavelengths, X-rays, to the longest, radio waves.

We know that if we rub a plastic comb against woollen material, it becomes charged. The comb will attract small pieces of paper. We call this an electric force. It was later realised that this attractive force is inversely proportional to the square of the distance separating the source of the force and the object attracted. (See appendix 3 also, note Newton's law of gravitation). But it was only in the twentieth century that technology had advanced to a stage where these processes could be studied and understood.

Lord Rutherford discovered that atoms were not elementary particles, but composite structures with internal parts. One of these is called the nucleus, which has an estimated diameter of one hundred billionth of a millimeter. It is surrounded by a cloud of smaller parts called electrons, from which quantum physics precludes detailed study.

Rutherford and Bohr discovered that electrons are bound to the nucleus by electric forces and that the nucleus is positively charged and surrounded by an electric field that holds the electrons in orbit. It was also discovered that the nucleus is a composite body containing two types of particles: protons (positively charged) and neutrons (electrically neutral).

Since the days of Rutherford and Bohr many advances have been made. The proton and neutron have been bashed with a view to bursting some of them open. A host of particles were released as a result. Protons were crashed into protons at high speed to determine what they contained. It was rather like bashing a common alarm clock with a hammer to see what was inside. In the case of protons crashing into one another, it was found that they were made up of smaller particles called quarks. Further investigation in a ''bubble chamber'' revealed that there are six types of quarks within the proton. They have been given the titles of: up, down, strange, charmed, bottom and top. It was as though bashing the alarm clock yielded a collection of wristwatches. These titles have arisen from the whims of individual physicists; they have no other significance.

Are quarks, then, the ultimate fundamental particles? Since the wavelength of light sets a limit to what one can see, reducing the wavelength and increasing the energy enables us to see a little more. But where does it stop? Quantum mechanics tells us that all particles in motion move in waves, and Heisenberg's uncertainty principle precludes us from viewing this phenomenon in greater detail.

The subatomic world is a very murky one, where common sense has no place and the unexpected and the undreamed of inevitably happen. Quantum effects rule supreme, and descriptive language that has meaning with respect to the macroworld has none in the subatomic world, which is uniquely strange despite our advanced knowledge.

Moreover, space was once considered a vast void in the blue deep, but research in the twentieth century shows that space is not empty. It is a place where much is going on and fundamental particles play innumerable tricks. Gerard Hooft of Utrecht discovered in 1971 a way to give meaning to the activity of such particles.

As stated above, four forces account for all known processes in the physical universe. They are listed in appendix 2, together with the particles they influence. Their range of action, their relative strengths, and the nature of the particles are indicated. Although the relative strengths are large, the distances over which they are effective are different.

The four known forces governing universal matter are:

1. **Gravity:** infinite in range, extremely weak within the atoms, and very strong in collapsed stars. Its chief role is that of binding planets, stars, and galaxies.
2. **Electromagnetic force:** author of light, life, and lightning. It is the cement that binds all ordinary materials together on this planet.
3. **The strong nuclear force** acts on protons and neutrons and binds the atomic nuclei and causes burning in stars, which, in turn, gives rise to an enormous release of energy, radiating into the universe for millions of years. The strong nuclear force is believed to be in the order of one hundred times the strength of the electric force; it acts on particles such as quarks. There is another consideration: the structure of nuclei is governed by the strong nuclear force, yet the structure of atoms is determined by the electromagnetic force. These extraordinary

systems, which govern the stability of protons and neutrons, we tend to take for granted; they are just "matter-of-fact." But if one dwells on such laws one must be alarmed.

4. **The weak force:** sometimes called the cosmic alchemist. It alters basic particles and causes some of the unstable nuclear particles to decay: for example, "pions" and "muons" disintegrate under the influence of the weak force (table B appendix 7). Such phenomena give rise to the disintegration of stars by bringing about a breakdown of particle bonding within the atom.

In 1973 at the Swiss laboratory in Berne, the weak force, or "star-burster," first revealed itself. Immediately the hunt was on in half a dozen countries—France, Belgium, Italy, Germany, and Britain now added to the United States, already working feverishly for years in the field—to understand it. As a result, many more fundamental particles now began to emerge. (A list is given in appendix 7.)

Richard Feynman, an eminent American physicist and inventor of the Feynman diagrams, devised a method by which particle activity could be understood and their elegance, beauty, and symmetry identified. Yuval Ne'eman from Israel and Murray Gell-Mann of Caltech also worked on the extraordinary symmetry of these subatomic particles.

It was the Japanese physicist Hideki Yukawa, however, who first found the basis of the symmetry. When he described the strong nuclear force, he explained, "the short-lived force-carrying particles, heavier than electrons but lighter than protons, come into being by drawing on borrowed energy permitted by the uncertainty principle. There is continuous interchange of energy between particles in space. They even change identity." (See figure 4, appendix 4.)

It is known, for example, that when a proton and neutron pass close to one another in space at high velocity the proton emits a pion (another fundamental particle), which is absorbed by the neutron. This activity results in changing a proton to a neutron or a neutron to a proton.

Such activities are common in high-energy physics, where little parcels of energy are exchanged or borrowed by one system and transferred to another. The time factors involved in such exchanges are in themselves quite benign in that such transfers have an extremely short duration—a few millionths of a second.

More advances, together with the development of highly sophisticated techniques, such as X-ray crystallography and powerful computers, are now making the subatomic world more amenable to study.

Order is evident throughout; physicists now refer to "a unique world of beauty, symmetry and harmony . . . exceeding man's wildest dreams."

We have seen that atoms are made of nuclei and electrons; nuclei are made of protons and neutrons. From protons and neutrons come mesons and quarks, some with "strangeness," others with "colour." Many other strange particles have made themselves known recently. (See table B, appendix 7.) The end is not in sight. It is not known what quarks contain; are they composite units? They certainly carry forces different, in nature and magnitude, from their parent particles—protons and neutrons.

One of the strangest and, for some, the least important particle discovered in recent times is the neutrino. Its existence was predicted by Wolfgang Pauli in 1930. It was not until 1956 that Fred Reiny and Clyde Cowan positively confirmed its existence. Suffice it to say that neutrinos are closely related to electrons but are lighter. They have extraordinary powers of penetration, and billions of them pass through our bodies as we read these words. By the time we think about them they are gone on their way through the Earth and out past the orbit of the moon to the stars.

Their function is in the process of radioactive decay, to which we shall refer later.

*　　*　　*

A flood of gifted men appeared from the 1890s onwards. They included J. J. Thompson, Ernest Rutherford, Albert Einstein, Werner Heisenberg, Max Börn, Niels Bohr, Louis de Broglie, Erwin Schrödinger, Enrico Fermi, Wolfgang Pauli, and Paul Dirac. The foundations of modern physics were laid by these men, and classical physics was turned on its head. Max Planck set them on their way in 1900, when he discovered that in a world in which matter comes in lumps (quantum) energy does likewise.

If the first decade of the twentieth century saw tremendous advances, it was not until the 1930s and 1940s that the world's most important discoveries in nuclear physics were really made—getting inside the nucleus and coming to terms with its contents.

An accurate description of the orbit of an electron is difficult; Niels Bohr did much to help. He was right in his predictions that the electron is obliged to whirl around the nucleus (keeping it from falling in on the nucleus) and yet radiate electromagnetic energy continuously. But he was wrong in assuming that the orbit of the electron was a simple one. In 1924 Louis de Broglie introduced the concept that the actual orbits of electrons and other particles in motion move in waves. The truth of de Broglie's findings was confirmed some years later: The orbit of an electron consists of vibrations similar to a closed wire loop. Any number of wavelengths formed around the loop fit wholly into the circumference of that loop, each wave joining smoothly with the next (figure 5).

It now became clear that a particle in motion moves in waves. The greater the particle's momentum, the shorter its

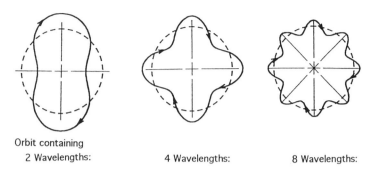

Orbit containing
2 Wavelengths: 4 Wavelengths: 8 Wavelengths:

Figure 5. Typical orbital radii in an atom.

wavelength. For example, an average-sized golf ball travelling at 30m/s will have a wavelength of 5.0×10^{-34} metres while an electron travelling at 107m/s will have a wavelength of 7.3×10^{-11} metres.

This characteristic is common to all matter in motion, including electrons orbiting the nuclei. When electrons are excited (energy added) they jump into larger orbits—orbits with greater radii. In doing so the circumference of the orbits increases; so does the number of wavelengths around the circumference. The wire-loop analogy holds good even with an increase in diameter of the loop. The extraordinary thing is that the increase in number of waves is a measure of the electron's energy level. There are other considerations that govern the excitation of atoms above the "ground state," that enables them to radiate their spectrum and thus disclose their nature or "fingerprint"; the absorption spectrum is one of these. Every element has a different spectrum—its fingerprint.

It was Niels Bohr who, with Rutherford's atom on one hand and the quantum theory on the other, had the genius to see where the next step lay: the spectrum of the atom is its fingerprint. While the atom is far too small to see with any instrument, Niels Bohr's imagination saw the atom through a stained-glass window, the absorption spectrum—that beautiful phenomenon that indicates what the electrons of that element are doing, either radiating or absorbing electromagnetic energy.

It is not proposed to go into nuclear processes, in detail, but a brief description of the atom may be helpful: all elements are made up of atoms, but each contains atoms of different atomic number and mass. For that reason, elements are given a special atomic number and mass.

For example: Hydrogen $_1H^2$

Sodium $_{11}Na^{23}$

Chlorine $_{17}Cl^{13}$

The general expression is: $_ZX^A$ where X is the name of the element Z the atomic number in the periodic table. It also indicates the number of electrons in a neutral atom and the number of protons within the nucleus. A is the mass number, that is, the number of neutrons and protons in the nucleus.

However, not all atoms of a particular element have exactly the same mass. Some don't even have the same number of neutrons in the nucleus as their sister atoms; in such cases they are called isotopes. Chlorine is an example. This element has two naturally occurring isotopes, $_{17}Cl^{35}$ and $_{17}Cl^{37}$. The former has seventeen protons and eighteen neutrons, the latter seventeen protons and thirty-seven neutrons. But their chemical properties are almost identical. It is a matter for reflection that an atom of a particular element can alter its mass number and preserve its properties. Chlorine is an example of how slight variations in the contents of the nucleus can occur. The reason for this is not known.

Suffice it to say that most elements have isotopes. Some

isotopes are naturally radioactive, and some can be made so by bombarding the nucleus with particles and rendering them unstable. Such techniques are now used as medical tools to trace the behaviour of substances in the body.

Chapter 8
Life

What is this thing called life? This mysterious property that most of us treasure and some abuse? Is it a force that drives animals and plants to get on with the business of living, or is it a very unique compound fired with something that enables us to grow, move, feed, and reproduce? Biologists do not consider replication adequate to define life; they insist that replication should not require an organism to import complex substances (proteins) to remain alive. The virus replicates itself when supplied with suitable substances from its host, but not otherwise. For that reason a virus is not considered to have independent life.

The ancients believed that life was a sort of working model of the soul that organised matter in animals and plants and disappeared at death.

In recent times it was recognised that electricity had something to do with life; electric shocks cause pain and twitching of muscles and can stop the heart. Nerves and muscles are sensitive to the electric force. Likewise, sensors attached to the skull record waves of electricity flowing across the brain, flowing at different rates for different mental activities.

Louis Pasteur realised that substances having left-handed and right-handed characteristics play an important role in the organisation of life.* This left-handedness and right-handedness

---

*Pasteur noticed in his study of life that the world is full of things whose right-handed version differs from the left-handed version. Each can be mirrored one in the other, but they cannot be turned in such a way that the right hand and

proved to be an important ingredient of life; a sample of living cells has this characteristic. We do not know exactly why life has this strange property.

Two discoveries in the twentieth century confirmed that chemistry is essentially a matter of the electrical behaviour of atoms and that inheritory instructions for life are embodied in a chemical code. So the electric force is related to life—it is also related to a spatial configuration of molecules when coupled together in a specific way. And what of the electric force that switches on the ignition of life? Can it be controlled or quantified? Biologists don't comment—they steer clear. Why?

We know that life has a number of strange ingredients in contrast to what was hitherto believed to be simple:

Complexity: The degree of complexity in living organisms exceeds that of any other physical system. This complexity ranges from the elaborate physical structure of molecules such as proteins and nucleic acid to that of delicate behaviour.

Uniqueness: Living organisms are distinctly unique in both form, activity, and development, which is totally unlike physics, where one studies classes of identical objects. Moreover, collections of organisms are unique, species are unique, and their evolution on Earth is unique.

Organisation: Organisms are not merely complicated; their complexity is beautifully organised and harmonised as a whole.

---

left hand become interchangeable. Pasteur then hit on the notion that there are also right-handed and left-handed molecules and that each had a function. He demonstrated this molecular characteristic by putting them into a solution and shining a polarised light (that is, light that will vibrate in one plane only) through them. The molecules of one kind (say, by convention, the molecules Pasteur called right-handed) rotated the plane of light to the left. Likewise for the left-handed molecules they rotated the plane of light to the right.

Holism: Living organisms are made up of a variety of individual components (for example, hair, eyes, bone, blood), yet these components behave as an integrated whole—they are all related and interdependent, one on the other. It used to be thought that life was a function of mechanistic forces that moved molecules in an orderly fashion from place to place. This view has fallen out of favour, and the holistic attribute is recognised.

Unpredictability: No living system exists in isolation; all are firmly coupled to their inanimate environment. They require a continual supply of matter (food) and energy. In addition, life on Earth is a network of mutually interdependent organisms which are in a continuous state of dynamic equilibrium.

Evolution: Life would not exist unless it had been able to evolve from simple to complex units. The ability of life-forms to evolve and adapt to change, develop more elaborate structures and functions, and transmit genetic information to their offspring are all uniquely characteristic of this ''thing'' called life.

Morphogenesis: Put simply, the problem is this: How is a disorganised collection of molecules assembled into a coherent whole that constitutes a living organism with all the right bits in the right places? Morphogenesis is remarkable in its robustness. The developing embryos of some species can be badly damaged in their early stages without affecting the end product. Embryos have the ability to ''regulate,'' which involves new cells replacing removed cells. There are organisms that can repair damage even in their adult form. Flatworms, for example, when chopped up develop into several complete worms; salamanders can regenerate an entire new limb if one is cut off.

There is a blueprint for all this, and the information is stored in the DNA of every cell. But how does a given cell know where it is located in relation to the remainder of the organism so as to adapt itself to suit the finished product? What is also surprising is the fact that although different parts of the organism develop differently, they all contain DNA. If every molecule of DNA possesses the same spatial configuration plan for the organism, how is it that different cells implement different parts of that very plan? Is there a superplan to signal to a cell the part it is to play in the overall plan? Certain genes within the DNA seem to be the governing factor. When it comes to understanding the mechanism controlling thought within the brain, we come up against the strange relationship of observer and the observed. This phenomenon becomes real when we come to the world of quantum physics.

Chapter 9
Ingredients of Life

Amino acids are the building blocks of proteins, which are the essential components of animal and plant tissue. (See figure 6, appendix 5.) There are about twenty amino acids in all. Their distribution is common throughout the animal and plant kingdoms. They have an ability to form linkages with one another in various combinations and permutations and, by so doing, form up to two hundred thousand known proteins. The linking arrangement of coding the acids is directed by DNA within the cell. The mechanism has a high intelligence content.

DNA is derived from nucleic acid, which has two forms, depending on the sugar content. They are deoxyribonucleic acid (DNA) and ribonucleic acid (RNA). DNA is a large molecular structure that takes the shape of a double helix in which the two strands consist alternatively of phosphate and sugar molecules. The two strands form a helix cross-linked at intervals by four nitrogenous bases, which are also derived from nucleic acid. (See figure 7.)

Throughout the life of a cell, coded instructions from the DNA are copied and used for protein manufacture. These copies, which are short strands of RNA, are interpreted by bodies called ribosomes, contained within the cell. The ribosomes move along the RNA strands and string together amino acids in accordance with the code given by DNA. The process is well documented

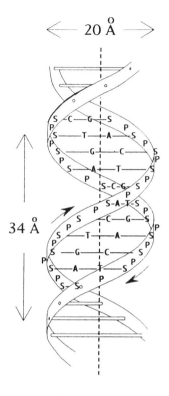

Figure 7. Watson-Crick model of DNA

in standard works in biochemistry; the essentials are all that matter here.

It is unnecessary for the reader to understand the chemistry employed by nature to form amino acids, enzymes, or proteins, just as it is unnecessary for one to understand the chemistry of petrol in order to be able to drive a car. The function of DNA is to replicate itself consistently and accurately throughout its life for the manufacturing of proteins within each cell. A simple analogy can be developed as follows. Imagine a set of railway tracks

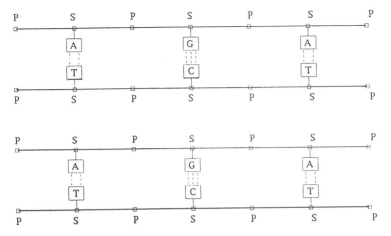

Figure 8. The DNA molecule uncoiled.

(the strands of the helix) made up of two lines of S and P molecules. (See figure 8.)

Imagine these tracks are cross-tied at the S intervals with "railway sleepers," which are analogous to nitrogenous based called adinine (A) thynine (T), guanine (G), and cytosine (C) molecules. This arrangement enables the "railway" to be turned upside down without altering its symmetry and chemical function. It so happens that in an ordinary railway, the sleepers are at approximately one-metre intervals. Therefore, a railway extending from New York to San Francisco would contain about 5 million sleepers. The "railway" in a single human cell contains approximately 6,000 million "sleepers," and the entire "track" is packed neatly inside each cell, which is less than one-hundredth of a millimetre in size. An extraordinary feature of the DNA molecule is its ability to copy itself accurately throughout its life.

Retaining the railway analogy a little further, the DNA molecule copies itself by cutting the "sleepers" in two and pushing the two halves of the tracks apart. The resulting gap is made good by sprouting two new half-sleepers each with a line of rails, thus ending up with two completely new railways, instead of the original one.

As stated earlier, some two hundred thousand different proteins are manufactured in the cells. They are all required at different times for different purposes. It is known that genes (a component of the DNA molecule) have to be "switched on" and "switched off" at various times when synthesising the proteins required; a complicated feedback mechanism achieves this.

The probability of even *one* protein (of the possible two hundred thousand different types), evolving at random without backup from correct stringing together of amino acids, coded by DNA, is estimated to be 1 in $10^{120,000}$, that is, 1 with 120,000 zeros added. Such a probability is, to all practical purposes, zero. It puts paid to the theory that "life occurred by chance in a primordial soup."

In fact, it is sometimes claimed by some that a veritable horde of monkeys hammering away on typewriters could eventually produce the plays of Shakespeare. This is wishful thinking by those who would like to believe that the origin of life happened by chance in a primordial soup.

There is another consideration: The human body contains approximately two thousands enzymes—proteins of high molecular weight. They have the specific function of speeding up natural chemical reactions in the body many hundreds of times, but they themselves do not participate in the reactions. They only accelerate them. They achieve this by making the "hand" of one reactant fit the "glove" of the other so that the two join forces and interact more readily. (See figure 9.)

It is a well-known fact that complex chemical reactions, involving synthesis and breakdown, are carried out more rapidly and easily by living organisms, at body temperature, than is possible in the laboratory under drastic conditions. In fact, many biologically occurring compounds have never been successfully

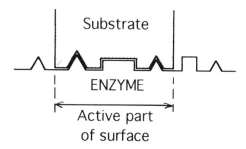

Figure 9. Diagrammatic representation of enzyme-substrate interaction.

made artificially. The reason is that such reactions are aided by catalysts or enzymes that only occur in living matter.

The existence of proteins brings us back to chains of amino acids in correct formation. Let us imagine the twenty amino acids comprising a string of twenty different-coloured beads. It is the order of these beads on the string that decides the type of a particular protein to be formed. Hundreds of ''beads'' of different colour combinations go to building a large protein molecule. In short, the order of the amino acids decides the protein; the DNA decides the amino acids.

We are back to probability: what is the probability of obtaining 2,000 individual enzymes by stringing amino acids together at random? The probability is, of course, 1 in $10^{160,000}$, which is unimaginably small. It is clearly a nonevent.

Since the probability of life evolving by chance is a nonevent, how did it evolve in the first instance? When one considers the odds of finding, at random, the amino acids coded to form 200,000 different proteins and 2,000 different enzymes, one has no alternative but to reject the claim that life originates by chance in ''organic soups.'' Either life requires a number of amino acids, proteins, and enzymes specifically coded, together with vitamins and electric potential, or it does not.

It is claimed that:

57

animal = chemical replication + electrical system.

If life requires such complex ingredients, from where do they originate? Stanley Miller and Harold Urey carried out an experiment in 1952 that supported the theory that life might originate from nonliving chemical substances—given enough time. Miller and Urey based their experiment on setting up conditions similar to those that obtained on the primordial Earth about 4,000 million years ago. The atmosphere at that time consisted of methane, ammonia, carbon dioxide, nitrogen, carbon monoxide, and hydrogen cyanide. There was no oxygen. Such conditions would be most hostile to life today. Anyway, Miller and Urey dissolved this concocted atmosphere in water and boiled it in a flask for days. Electric discharges were then pushed through it to simulate lightning. The mixture darkened. When tested, it was found to contain a few amino acids. They repeated the tests under varying conditions, but always with the same results.

Later, Dr. Orgel carried out a number of similar experiments, but instead of boiling the mixture, he froze it. As a result the concentrated material formed a tiny iceberg containing organic molecules—a few amino acids and one of the four nitrogenous bases of DNA appeared. Many experiments similar to those of Miller and Orgel have since been carried out. They all produced the same results—three or four amino acids under the most encouraging conditions. But this is a far cry from the series of amino acids (the beads on the string) that are required and coded by DNA to make a *single* protein molecule. Before coding anything, one DNA helix must first be in place. So we require the four nitrogenous bases together with the sugar and phosphate strands, all built in to produce one DNA molecule complete; we also require the twenty amino acids formed and coded to meet the enormous protein requirements of a living organism. We then require thousands of enzymes to encourage appropriate chemical reactions. Hundreds of amino acid combinations are also required to make one protein! Again there is zero chance of success.

It is argued that primitive life hardly requires the numbers of amino acids, proteins, and enzymes that higher species require, but this only marginally improves the impossible odds of life occurring at random in any terrestrial conditions.

There is another way to look at this universal mystery: Amino acids have a unique spatial configuration across the face of biology. As soon as we calculate the probability of the configuration being correct for a given series of acids, to form one protein nucleotide, we find the numbers become astronomically large. Put another way: If we were to assume one nucleotide every million generations, how long does 1 million new generations take to form?

Fred Hoyle believes that "we are looking at something of cosmic scale when we examine the biochemistry of life; for that reason one had a situation that was more powerful than the terrestrial one by something in the order of 10^{20}, which is an enormous increase in magnitude. But that does not seem sufficient," he claims. "I am overwhelmed by the complexity of life form. If you say to me that you can have the whole of our galaxy and all the galaxies you can see, I still cannot see how any form of shuffling by natural processes can produce the system involving life itself."

Hoyle is satisfied that there is "an information content" in the universe that is enormous, as indicated in living systems, and that the short time scale for the whole universe is quite inadequate to provide for that information content. He continues:

> I would even go so far as to say that almost all that is seen in the universe is a product of intelligence, for example, stone walls up the side of a mountain; roads, bridges, canals; birds' nests, fertilisation, growth, etc., all of these have the ingredients of natural processes but they also have the ingredients of intelligence.

Hoyle now believes that the explanation for this ''intelligence content'' is that of ''a hidden hand.'' Fred Hoyle is not a believer in God, but he says he is now searching for God.

Chapter 10
Evolution

Charles Darwin (1809–82) published *The Origin of the Species* in 1859. It was an instant sensation and a best-seller. The essence of the theory is that "nature acts as a selective force, killing off the weak and forming new species from the survivors who are fitted to their environment."

Alfred Russel Wallace, a naturalist fifteen years Darwin's junior, after spending a period with Indian tribes in the Amazon Basin wrote:

> Natural selection could only have endowed savage man with a brain a few degrees superior to that of an ape, whereas he actually possesses one very little inferior to that of a philosopher. With our advent there had come into existence a being in whom that subtle force we term "mind" became of far more importance than mere bodily structure.

The twentieth century saw Darwin's theory of evolution challenged, undermined, and discredited. For over a century the theory was popular; it was swallowed hook, line, and sinker by the "enlightened" of the time. It became holy writ, the gospel according to Mr. Darwin, accepted by all and vigorously defended by many. But its attractiveness was based more on social changes and historical circumstances than on the theory itself, rife with error. To begin with, Darwin was not the first to conceive the idea. Classical biology began with the discovery of the microscope in 1673 by Antonie van Leeuwenhoek. This enabled living matter to be examined in detail.

With the coming of industrialisation and the prospect of increased prosperity for all, a greater demand for knowledge ensued. Progress was resisted by the Church and by established patterns of society. This movement for learning had its origins in France, where the first logical evolutionary theory, of Jean-Baptiste de Lamarck (1744–1829), arose. Lamarck reasoned that characteristics acquired by parents are transmitted to their offspring. The method by which this took place was not known, but it was conceded this theory had a logical ring to it. Consider animals, for example, that feed on the leaves of trees. They constantly have to stretch higher and higher. The result is, according to Lamarck, that the offspring will be born with progressively longer necks. If this were to be repeated often enough the result could well be a giraffe, but for DNA control.

Lamarck's theory was shown to be false. Nature requires a change in the genetic structure before the bodily characteristics of the animal alter, not the other way round. No amount of muscular activity on the part of the animal, however, can work its way backwards to the detailed structure of the DNA double helix, which carries the genetic information of structure. Should this have been possible, extremes in everything would become inevitable and reach bizarre proportions, when every physiological requirement of a particular species could be met with a little practice.

The eighteenth century was unusually active in biological and geological sciences. The French had sown seeds indicating that time was, in some way, related to evolution; the true age of the Earth was now in question. Many of the beliefs of the comfortable establishments such as the Church were now being discredited.

Hitherto conservative religions had insisted that the biblical time scale of a few thousand years indicated the Earth's age, but the work of geologists James Hutton (1726–97) and Charles Lyell (1797–1875) from a study of rock formations showed that the Earth was, in fact, millions of years old. In 1835, Edward Blyth published *The Varieties of Animals,* which indicated the first understanding of a genetic structure in every living form. Blyth believed that natural selection operated on the various species. He gave no explanation as to how the various species came to be present in the first place but suggested that ''special creation'' was a plausible explanation.

By the 1850s industrialisation in France and Britain was in full swing. Conservative elements of society were fighting a losing battle; ordinary workers saw the dawn of enlightenment breaking. It only takes a tiny spark to set off a bonfire if the fuel is right. Darwin's *Origin of the Species* was such fuel for the fire of the Victorian age. It explains why *Origin* was initially such an instant success.

Darwin's work, however, contained much that was already available; it contained no original thinking. The material in *Origin* was presented as proof of his theory, but in fact it is nothing more than evidence of the existence of evolution, not evidence of its cause. The French had been convinced of the existence of evolution a century before Darwin—two centuries before him, if Robert Hooke is given credit.

Moreover, there is not a shred of evidence in the fossil record to support Darwin's theory of evolution. A fatal misconception of Darwin's supporters, after the publication of *Origin* was the belief that the fossil record supported the theory. There was no evidence that changes in the genetic structure occurred, step-by-step, in the fossil record, such as the transition from reptiles to mammals or the transition from wingless to winged insects. No such step in the gradual transition has ever been found. Indeed, the process is the opposite to what the theory predicts. Small variations do exist, but they do not accumulate, step-by-step, into major changes. So where major changes have occurred they must have done so by sudden jumps—so quickly as *not* to be recorded in the fossil record. (See figure 10.) This is the essence of the matter; this is the rock on which Darwin's theory founders.

In the meantime, research came face to face with a cogent and telling reality: The driving forces in evolution lie in the source of the variations on which natural selection operates. Biologists have now come to terms with the mechanisms of heredity, that is, the copying of the DNA code. When mistakes do occur in the mechanism, that is, miscopying of the code, changes in the amino acid chains have taken place, resulting in changes in proteins and cell chemistry. But are such mistakes significant? One of the wonders of the modern world is the accuracy with which the DNA code is copied and passed on to the next generation. It is the accuracy of the actual copying process that is the unique feature of DNA. It limits variations in natural selection to an absolute minimum. Should the copying process not have been accurate, infinite variations would arise and chaotic messages would be coded and transmitted.

Let us take an example. Consider a long string of differently coloured beads (amino acids) representing a particular protein. Suppose we inadvertently alter the position of one bead on the string. It will give rise to a mutation in the structure of the intended protein. It would not be unreasonable to make such a mistake, especially if we were asked to string the correct colours together quickly. One could imagine large room for error if we were asked to make copies of some 200,000 different strings (different proteins) and, because of injury to a particular individual, urgency was essential. An enormous number of errors would arise. Yet the body does this job within the cells millions of times per day, but the number of mistakes is extremely few.

The process by which evolution takes place has, in the opinion of anthropologists and biologists, been reduced to one of two possibilities.
Either

1. Darwin's theory that evolution proceeds at a slow and relatively constant rate is correct; *or*
2. evolution proceeds by abrupt changes followed by long periods or plateaux of stability—the modern view. (See figure 10.)

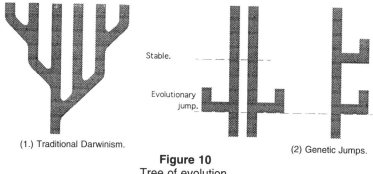

(1.) Traditional Darwinism.

Stable.

Evolutionary jump.

(2) Genetic Jumps.

Figure 10
Tree of evolution.
(1) Slow at constant rate.   (2) abrupt change

This has recently been borne out in a study of fossils. The theory was first enunciated by N. Eldridge and S. J. Gould in 1972 under the title of "punctuated equilibria." There is increasing evidence to support it.

Supporters of Darwin's theory didn't like the "punctuated equilibria" theory, as it completely undermined the "slow, relatively constant rate theory," which they believed was caused by mutation or random drift. In other words, the frequent mistakes claimed by Darwin in copying the DNA code constituted the foundation stone of the theory. As outlined above, recent studies and statistical probability have now shown the errors here are extraordinarily few having regard to the billions of cells that replicate every minute daily. If one comes to think of it, there would have to be extraordinarily few mistakes in the copying process if the animal and plant kingdoms are to avoid bizarre inherited variations and subsequent annihilation.

Neo-Darwinism failed because random variations tend to worsen performance, not improve it. The theory provides no explanations as to how the genetic information got here in the first place. The probability of such a complex and orderly system evolving by chance on the Earth's surface is inconceivably small, even over billions of years. It is, as has been said, as probable as a horde of monkeys thumping away on typewriters to produce Shakespeare's plays.

When all is said and done concerning the origin of life on Earth, when the probability of stringing the correct permutation and combination of amino acids together to form 200,000 proteins and 2,000 enzymes is calculated, the chance of such intricate events occurring at random is outside reason and probability.

Darwin knew nothing about the replication mechanism, nor did he know of the structure or the ingenuity of DNA coding. Notwithstanding, he had many doubts about much that he claimed as fact in his *Origin of the Species,* and he said so. He knew his work would cause soul-searching. But deep within him there were grave doubts as to the truth of his work and his conviction.

As a person, Darwin was sombre and full of misgivings due to lack of quality thinking and an inbuilt fear that his theories were not correct. He delayed putting down his thoughts on paper for four years and only got the courage to do so after having read Thomas Malthus's *Essay on Population.* In this work Malthus put forward the idea that population multiplies faster than food and if that is true of animals, then they must compete to survive. Here was Darwin's excuse to carry on. When he had finished his work he became scared and asked his wife to publish it after his death. He was also a hypochondriac, taking frequent refuge in bottles of medicine and living in a house without ventilation. His wife was known to have had a difficult time as a result.

Today the evidence that evolution occurs in jumps separated by long intervals of stability is overwhelming. We might study the evidence as to why evolution behaves in such a manner, proceeding as it does in a stop-and-go fashion.

Chapter 11
Life Outside Our Planet

Stars are millions of millions of miles from us; the nearest is Alpha Centauri, which is 4.2 light-years, that is, 24 million million miles, away, so that a rocket from Earth, travelling at a velocity of a practicable order, would take millions of years to reach it.

We do not know if the stars have solar systems or planets that could support life. The most powerful telescopes available are not quite good enough to determine this. But there is indirect evidence that some stars have planetary systems; the existence of planets can, however, be deduced from a study of a star's motion relative to a fixed point.

In early times man regarded stars as tiny lamps in the celestial dome. They did not know then that stars are, in fact, gigantic atomic furnaces that form the elements within their cores.

But what of this universe, this conglomerate of millions of galaxies, each rotating, spinning, and receding from us and from one another at velocities that are slowing down? In fact, each galaxy is made up of millions of atomic furnaces, each of which explodes or contracts when mature; each is a beacon of light, energy, and power. Whence has all this come?

Origin of the Universe

The origin of the universe has been the subject of speculation from early times. There are numerous theories as to its origin, but only three have survived: (1.) the big bang theory; (2.) the oscillation theory; and (3.) the steady state theory. These may be summarised as follows:

The Big Bang Theory

This theory was proposed by George Gamow in 1924. It provides answers to which most scientists, including astronomers, now subscribe. It states that the initial condition of the universe was a superconcentration of primeval hydrogen that exploded 18,000–20,000 million years ago and yielded the ingredients of matter. (The theory does not explain where the "primeval hydrogen" came from.) The current expansion of the galaxies is believed to be the remaining impetus of that very explosion. From the searing violence that accompanied the explosion and the creation of space, time, and light, relics of the explosion still survive. The most important of these are as follows:

1. The low level of radiation coming from space, as discovered by Penzias and Wilson.
2. Evidence of a uniformly expanding universe.
3. Fusion of hydrogen nuclei to form helium and deuterium.
4. Eighteen to 20 billion years on, the temperature of the universe has dropped to three degrees above absolute zero ($-273°C$). Knowing the current temperature, therefore, it is relatively easy to work back and compute the temperatures at all epochs.
5. Using modern particle accelerators, it is possible to generate high-energy particle collisions and simulate conditions that obtained a split second after the big bang. This has been done. Experiments show that the temperature initially had been a staggering million billion degrees.

6. Recent evidence of weak but regular gravitational waves or ripples in the curvature of space travel at the speed of light. They are similar to light waves, which are ripples of the electromagnetic field. But the gravitational waves are much harder to detect. They appear to be the remnants of the enormous waves of energy that resulted from the big bang.
7. The existence of "dark matter" that occupies some 80 percent of space. The nature of this material is unknown, but its influence on the force of gravity is well established. It does not include cosmic particles.
8. The second law of thermodynamics, stating that the universe is becoming increasingly disordered and gradually running down.

There are many other proofs of the occurrence of the big bang, but this will suffice.

The Oscillation Theory

This theory was proposed by Abbé Georges Henri Lemaître in 1927. It suggests that at intervals, from 60,000 million years to 25,000 million years, all matter in the universe comes together. This is followed by a universal explosion, which does not continue indefinitely. It is then followed by a new phase of contraction, ending with all the material coming together once more. On the basis of this theory, the universe may have existed for an indefinite time. Why it should systematically expand and contract without a change in overall energy has not been explained.

The Steady State Theory

This theory was postulated in 1948 by Herman Bondi, T. Gold, and Fred Hoyle at Cambridge. It proposes that new matter is being created continuously out of nothing in the form of hydrogen atoms. According to the theory, the rate of such creation is too slow to be detected, but as existing galaxies separate and pass beyond the boundary of the observable universe, new galaxies are formed from the freshly created material, the result being that the overall aspect of the universe will always be the same. According to the theory, there was no moment of creation: the universe always existed and always will.

The last two of the above theories have been abandoned.

Let us now examine one of the billions of stars in the universe, our sun. Enough is known about star formation to understand that there is an underlying pattern governing the process. The laws of physics, as we know them, are a vital part of the process, a process where condensation, gravitation, temperature, pressure, and heat are concerned.

There is overwhelming evidence that we live in an **ordered universe,** which is governed by simple mathematical laws, from the smallest atom to the largest galaxy. Our solar system must have evolved when the expanding debris from a nearby supernova explosion passed through vast clouds of gas and dust approximately 4.70 million years ago. The shock waves from the explosion caused the collapse of those clouds. Gravity then pulled the condensed particles together. The accumulated material gradually increased in density and temperature and formed a rotating disc of gas and dust, which eventually heated to enormous temperatures and pressures. The core of that disc became the sun. (Models of this process are well understood.) The outer layer of the disc formed the planets and satellites, together with asteroids and comets, all of which form systems similar to ours.

With the cooling of the disc, the materials that emerged from the initial explosion condensed and gave rise to silicates, metals, iced water, carbon dioxide, methane, and ammonia. These materials collided and coalesced and grew into large bodies. The finer materials were pushed into space by the "solar wind," which is a continuous outflow of atomic particles from the sun.

Four terrestrial or Earth-like planets occupy the inner part of our solar system. Each is a solid sphere with a metallic core surrounded by a shell of silicates. The giant planets Jupiter, Saturn, Uranus, and Neptune consist predominantly of gas, with little rocky material. Yet these four contain almost 95 percent of all material in our solar system.

A belt of asteroids, or minor planets, orbit the sun between Mars and Jupiter. The largest of these is about one thousand kilometers in diameter but most of the other 2,200 known asteroids are smaller.

There is yet another group of bodies, called meteorites, which also orbit the sun. Their orbits are elliptical. They sweep in around the sun and then out beyond the orbit of Saturn and the rest of the planets.

Then there are the comets, those mysterious and beautiful objects that sweep the night sky on their way from the depths of space. Comets have tails that extend over large stretches of sky, sometimes reaching from zenith to horizon. In olden times comets were considered omens; advances in astronomy put an end to such superstition. Comets are believed to be fragments of the solar system that have broken loose and journeyed deep into space, traversing orbits that take them thousands of years to complete. They are small compared with other celestial bodies—the largest comet may have a diameter of twenty kilometres.

As comets approach and swing around the sun in their orbits, rock and other friable material become visible in the form of long tails. Chemical analyses of the material forming those tails indicate that their most common constituents are hydrogen, carbon, nitrogen, and oxygen. These are also the elements that are most common in living material. Moreover, it is known that the relative number of atoms of these four elements is almost identical in comets and in living matter. Hoyle and others pointed out that "this characteristic is not shared by material from any other astronomical source, even from the earth's atmosphere and oceans."

Professor Delsemme of the University of Toledo, Ohio, has calculated the relative abundance of elements in comets and living matter. He found that the evaporated material of comets contains far more carbon and nitrogen in proportion to hydrogen and oxygen than in the biosphere. He also found that the proportion of those elements in bacteria and in mammals is unmistakably similar to that in comets.

It is Fred Hoyle's opinion that "it does not make too much difference what particular life-form one looks at; the proportions of the four vital elements are always the same and more in accordance with evaporated material of comets than that of earth's atmosphere."

It is known that the Earth has been struck many times by large objects from outer space. There is evidence of this in a number of places on Earth. An unusually heavy rain of such objects occurred 65 million years ago, which happens to correspond with the extinction of dinosaurs. Some believe that the extinction was not confined to dinosaurs, but included all sizeable animals on earth, because of lengthy diminution of sunlight due to dust clouds. Others believe that the objects from space bore poisonous material to Earth; this seems implausible. We may never know the truth.

The chance of finding the remains of celestial bodies that collided with our Earth is remote, but some have been found. A shower fell in 1864 near Orgenil, France, and some fell in Tanzania in 1938. There was also one in Murchison, Victoria, Australia, in 1969. Samples of each of these have been examined by scientists such as G. Claus, B. Nagy, Harold Urey, and Hans Pflug. There is unanimity that the remains of life from outside the Earth were identified in each.

From his experience of micro-organisms Hans Pflug identified similarities between the fossilized remains contained in these materials and the terrestrial bacterium *pedomicrobium*. In addition to locating evidence of bacteria in meteorites, Pflug found fossilised remains of other structures that are similar to the viruses found on Earth. It is evident that the fossils of micro-organisms can get to Earth on board meteorites and other rock fragments thrown onto our planet from great distances out, but how about living organisms such as bacteria getting here?

If micro-organisms, such as bacteria, are to penetrate the Earth's atmosphere successfully and not burn up on the way, they must be able to survive massive doses of radiation in space. Radiation damages the genetic machinery of the cell and renders its coding system useless. But since radiation, in the form of low-energy-X-rays from stars, pervades space, how then do micro-organisms survive? Again nature foresaw the difficulty and came up with the answer: Micro-organisms happen to be endowed with an extraordinary ability to repair themselves with the help of the enzymes that they contain. Their ability to repair themselves has been tested in recent times during space flights and in laboratories. It has been found that micro-organisms survive enormous variations in temperature, pressure, and radiation and, what is more intriguing, the organisms are designed for such conditions. This signifies that they have cosmic dimensions and are not confined to Earth.

There is another aspect to this phenomenon: It was noted earlier (see page 49) that we can have left-handed or right-handed molecules. Many amino acids take one or other forms, but all living organisms generally use the left-handed form. Curiously, the Murchison meteorite was found to contain amino acids that were also left-handed, indicating that the origin was biological.

Chapter 12
The Origin of Life

A new phenomenon, in relation to life, came to light in the 1960s. It has profound implications.

It is known that interstellar space contains vast quantities of "dust," in addition to enormous quantities of cosmic particles and atoms. The presence of the dust had long been a source of wonder and nuisance to astronomers—nuisance because it prevented them from obtaining an uninterrupted view into most of the celestial deep. It was thought that the "fog" or "dust" consisted of particles of water ice. In 1979, however, Fred Hoyle and Chandra Wickramasinghe cracked that mystery. They used techniques that proved that the dust was, in fact, of biological origin.

Samples of the dust were collected, analysed, and tested for resistance to extremes in temperature and radiation. The question was: could these particles, if organic, resist the temperatures of entry through our atmosphere? Accordingly, a number of balloon ascents were made in the United States during the mid-1960s. They reached the top of the stratosphere (thirty miles up). The Soviets later carried out more stringent tests at heights well into the ionosphere—fifty miles up. The tests confirmed that life exists at levels well above the reach of air movement of any kind.

A large amount of scientific information was collected between 1979 and 1989 by U.S. and Soviet space flights. Many experiments were carried out to detect the chemical activity of living matter on other planets. The experiments showed that traces of life did exist on other planets. As we have seen, there is a vast quantity of supporting evidence from fossil records taken from meteorites that crashed into the Earth at one time or another. The analysis of the gases emitted from comets was also confirmatory.

Scientists, including astronomers, are now inclined to the view that the origin of life lies outside the Earth and not on it. The work of such men as N. Eldredge, S. Gould, G. Claus, Hans Pflug, and B. Nagy expounds on this view. Hoyle sums up the position succinctly:

> The origin of life and its formation content did not arise on earth. Nor, despite widespread belief in the work of Darwin, did terrestrial life evolve in the way he suggested. Yet, evolution certainly has occurred—there can be no doubt about that—but in a way that is prompted from a very different source than the one imaged by earth-bound theory.

Hoyle is here referring to the "primordial soup" theory. Where does this leave us? It opens a vista of infinite proportions and intelligence:

> The presence of micro organisms in space and on other planets and their ability to survive a journey through the earth's atmosphere point to one conclusion: they make it highly likely that the genetic material of cells—the DNA double helix—is an accumulation of genes that arrive on earth from outside. This theory avoids the devastating impossibility facing anyone who seeks to maintain an earth centred picture of the origin of life and it also avoids the faulty logic of Darwinism.

In short, the evidence is there to support the belief that micro-organisms can readily reach the Earth's surface from outer regions.

Microbiology is the study of micro-organisms* too small to be seen with the unaided eye. An object with a diameter less than one-tenth of a millimeter cannot clearly be perceived by the unaided eye, and very little detail can be seen in an object with a diameter of one millimeter. Organisms with a diameter of one millimeter, or less, are therefore included in microbiological study. They have an enormous range and distributions on Earth. They include metazoan animals, protozoa, algae and fungi, bacteria, and viruses. The existence of such a vast living world was unknown until the invention of the microscope.

The first person to recognise their existence was a Dutch merchant, Antonie van Leeuwenhoek (1632–1723), whose scientific activities fitted his business affairs. He was no exception—for the greatest discoveries in all fields of science in those days were made by amateurs who earned their living in other ways. Leeuwenhoek was remarkable in that he had little formal education and never attended a university—which was probably a good thing in many ways. Nevertheless, he was endowed with extraordinary skills in microscope observations. All the main kinds of unicellular microorganisms known today—protozoa, algae, yeast, and bacteria—were first described by him with surprising accuracy.

After Leeuwenhoek had discovered the existence of vast numbers of microscopic objects, scientists began to wonder about their origin. Some believed that "the little creatures were formed spontaneously from non-living materials"; others (Leeuwenhoek included) believed that they were formed from the "seeds" or "germs" of those creatures that were always present in the air. The first of these theories, known as "spontaneous generation,"

---

*Micro-organisms are today assumed to have split away or diverged from all other forms of life at a stage when there had been no division into plants and animals. A rational approach is to regard micro-organisms as not belonging to either plant or animal kingdom, but forming a third and clearly distinct kingdom of protists.

survived until the Renaissance. It was abandoned as a result of the work of an Italian physician, Francesco Redi, in 1665. He showed that the maggots developed in putrefying meat are the larval stages of flies and would never appear if the meat had been protected in the first instance. However, spontaneous generation died a slow death; the concept struggled on in the minds of biologists until well into the nineteenth century. The distinguished work of Louis Pasteur (1822–1895) finally put an end to the theory of spontaneous generation.

Pasteur grew up in the town of Arbois in the French Jura. It was a place he loved and returned to each year. He reached the height of his powers in 1863 (he was then forty) when the emperor of France asked him to examine what went wrong with the fermentation of wine. "Wine is a sea of organisms," said Pasteur. "By some it lives; by some it decays." Pasteur was the first to find organisms that live without oxygen. This fact at the time was a nuisance to winegrowers but since then had turned out to be vital to the understanding of the beginning of life. It was then that the Earth was without oxygen.

But what are these micro-organisms and why did they receive such attention? In 1864 a young British surgeon, Joseph Lister, discovered that surgical sepsis could be substantially reduce if scrupulous sterilisation of surgical instruments was carried out and disinfected dressings used. Moreover, operations performed under a spray of disinfectant also produced good results. This was the first direct evidence for the germ theory of disease, even thought it cast no light on the microbial cause of specific diseases.

Conclusive proof of the cause of disease was provided in 1876 by Robert Koch, a German country physician. He had no laboratory, and his experiments were conducted in his home, using primitive equipment and small experimental animals. He showed that mice could be infected with anthrax from a diseased domestic animal, transmitting the infection through a series of twenty mice by successive inoculations. He then proceeded to cultivate the causative bacterium by introducing minute heavily infected particles of spleen from a diseased animal into drops of sterile serum. Having observed, hour by hour, the growth of the organisms in the culture, he saw the rods changed into long filaments within each ovoid; refractile bodies appeared. He showed that these bodies were spores. Spores had never been seen before, yet they had existed since life on Earth began. So anthrax was the disease with which Koch made his name in history.

Koch carried out many other experiments demonstrating the biological specificity of disease agents and eventually concluded that "only one kind of bacillus can cause this specific disease process, while other bacteria either do not produce disease following inoculation, or give rise to other kinds of disease."

Work on anthrax ushered in the golden age of medical bacteriology when new institutes were founded in Paris and Berlin for Pasteur and Koch.

Pasteur's institute developed filters that would retain bacterial cells. Later it was learned that disease could still get through the filter even though all bacteria had been retained, and so viruses were discovered! Suffice it to say that whole families of micro-organisms were now emerging and the role that each played, as agents of infectious diseases, became central to biology at the end of the nineteenth century. The role of micro-organisms in the fixation of atmospheric nitrogen, as a source for living organisms, was also discovered at that time. The vital role that such organisms play in the cycles of matter on Earth such as the cycles of carbon, nitrogen, and sulphur became evident. It was these groups that carried out essential chemical transformations in plants and animals and enabled them to grow. Another of the many marvels of nature was revealed. It had its beginning as the twentieth century dawned.

For half a century after the death of Louis Pasteur, microbiology and general biology developed independently. Microbiology concentrated on the cause of infectious diseases, and the study of immunity. General biology confined its studies to the organisation of animal and plant cells and their role in reproduction and development. It was then that the study of heredity and evolution commenced. A big step in the study of the science of life had begun.

The discovery of cell-free alcoholic fermentation by H. Buchrer in 1897 was the next step. It provided the key to chemical analysis of energy-yielding metabolic processes. Buchrer accidentally found, when attempting to preserve an extract of yeast prepared by grinding the cells with sand, that when he added sugar to the mix, carbon dioxide was liberated and the formation of alcohol occurred. A soluble enzyme capable of carrying out alcoholic formation was thus discovered. Its implications were far-reaching.

Biochemistry rapidly advanced on the strength of such work, simple though it may appear today. The fundamental similarity of the mechanisms of glycolysis (forming sugar) by muscle and alcoholic fermentation by yeast (a sugar) became apparent. Physiologists and microbiochemists had found common ground. A few years later the analysis of animal and microbial nutrition found another common denominator: the vitamin, an essential requirement of animal life. It proved to be chemically identical to the ''growth factor'' also required by bacteria and yeasts. A study of these substances revealed that they are forerunners of groups of enzymes that play indispensable roles in the metabolism of the cell.

The next advance was around the corner: the discipline of genetics resulting from the convergence of cytology (study of animal cells) and Mendelian analysis. Initially it had little impact. Hitherto it was doubtful if the inheritance mechanism in plants and animals also functioned in bacteria. The work of Max Delbrück and Salvador Luria in 1943 provided the first step in the proof; Avery McLeod and McCarthy in 1944 provided the second. They discovered the nature of hereditary material in bacteria. A linkup of the processes and mechanisms employed by nature in the living cells had been established.

Chapter 13
The Living Cell

The ingredients of life have captivated man's interest from early times. But because of their complexity, little progress in understanding their nature was made until recent times. For thousands of years man has confined himself to classifying, recording, and comparing living species, but never coming to grips with what life itself is. The subject became so much of a puzzle and a conundrum that it was not even fashionable to discuss the question. Life was just a "mystery" and left at that. Such an approach evades the question.

With the twentieth century and the development of the electron microscope it became evident that beneath the bewildering diversity of life-forms there is a unity at microscopic and biochemical levels, a unity that transcends everything that life represents—the cell, often called the atom of biology.

The average animal or plant cell has an overall dimension of one thousandth of a millimeter across. It is sack-shaped and surrounded by a cell membrane that has a thickness of approximately 75 hundredths of a millimeter. (See figure 3.)

The cell is filled with a jellylike substance (cytoplasm) in which are suspended the nucleus and nucleolus together with a number of other specialised subcellular structures such as mitochrondia, ribosomes, centrosomes, Golgi bodies, and canals that extend from the nucleus to the surface of the sac wall. All these structures have specific functions and are always active. Mitochondria, for example, are called the powerhouse of the cell;

ribosomes are the seats of protein synthesis. Recent studies indicate that the mitochondria, which is transmitted by the mother of the species, was once entirely independent of the cell. Studies in Berkeley, California, have shown that mitochondria can be used to trace the origin and age of man.

Cells do not die; they increase in size and at a predetermined moment, which cannot be predicted, divide into two daughter cells. This multiplication is first preceded inside the parent cell by a division of the nucleus. (See figure 11, page 88.)

The nucleus is the essential feature of the cell. It consists of large molecules of DNA. It is the "master file" that stores the blueprint needed for replication referred to previously. This blueprint contains the specification for every component of the cell. It specifies when and how each component should be manufactured and assembled so as to recreate a similar cell. Libraries of books exist describing how this extraordinary but, nonetheless, ingenious work is carried out. It will suffice to describe the results in the briefest terms.

Heredity is the process by which mice, men, buttercups, and bacteria reproduce themselves. It is the essential feature of life; it is that which makes for continuity in every species of both animal and plant. Should it go wrong, commencing with the probability of an error as small as one part in a million in a given species, it would not be long before the species would be entirely extinct or have evolved into something else. It is said that heredity holds the promise of immortality in the perpetuation of a species. The method by which it accomplishes this is of interest.

Genetics is the science of heredity and involves the study of the variations by which offspring differ from being exact copies of their parents. The differences between parents and offspring are sometimes obvious, such as colour of eyes and hair; this is also true of plants, with variations in such things as the colour of flowers; and, in bacteria in the ability to flourish in the presence of antibiotic drugs. Differences that are less obvious are also numerous but subtle; for example, the manner in which one speaks or walks or reacts to particular stimuli.

How are all these characteristics transmitted from parent or grandparent? We know family characteristics are transmitted to a greater or lesser extent from generation to generation. The irony is that nature does the job with unusual accuracy.

Gregor Mendel (1822–84) showed the hereditary traits of the individual are distinctive and are transmitted as independent and separate units from parents to offspring. Each parent contributes about 50 percent of the characteristics of the offspring at time of mating. While individuals possess distinctive traits that characterise them, each trait is controlled by an individual unit called a gene, which is also a protein and lies on the chromosomes in the nucleus of the cell. (See figure 11.)

Gregor Mendel was a farmer's son from Brünn (now Brno), in Czechoslovakia. The family was very poor, and Gregor, anxious to get a bit of education, entered the Augustinian Order in his own town as a lay brother. The abbot decided to send Mendel to the University of Vienna to get a diploma in teaching, as the monastery was a teaching centre. Mendel's mind was far from teaching; his interests were elsewhere. Accordingly, he was not a success in Vienna and asked to be taken home to the monastery to work in the garden. He was used to farm work. He saw in the growing of plants ''an order and a discipline.'' He had been brooding much and admiring much in biology.

While in Vienna he was greatly influenced by one of his lecturers, Franz Unger, who took a keen interest in the subject of inheritance. Unger did so in a most practical way. ''Sow the seeds; study the results,'' he would frequently say. Mendel was fascinated by him. If Vienna did nothing else for young Mendel, it put him on the road to resolving his great problem! *What is it that makes us so like our parents and so different, so like our grandparents and so different? We are the mosaic of our ancestors, and why?* Mendel had dark, ponderous thoughts, so much so that when beginning his studies of garden peas he guessed that peas had seven individual characteristics, no less and no more. His guess was right, even though there was nothing known about genes in his day. This was genius. Out of the thousands of experiments he then carried out in breeding peas came his now famous laws in genetics. He published a paper on his findings; nobody was interested then. They didn't understand his work. Two years later he was promoted to abbot of the monastery; it was said at the time that the bishop and some other clergy did not approve of his work and "promoted him sideways." He still found time, as abbot, apart from looking after the finances of the monastery, to breed a strain of honeybees that stung all round them. The bees had to be destroyed! He died in 1884 a great favourite of the other monks. The great Czech composer Leoš Janáček played the organ at Mendel's funeral. His work of genius was only discovered in a local library in 1900 by an American biologist. From then on Mendel would be immortal.

Genes are conveyed to offspring by their parents in a manner that is governed by "chance." But chance, as mentioned earlier, is a far-reaching phenomenon. We use the word when we do not understand why or how a particular process occurs.

An illustration of the method used by nature in the inheritance process will serve to demonstrate chance: A brown-eyed person may differ from a blue-eyed person by a single gene, so that the gene controlling eye colour exists in one of two alternative forms. Let us use B to represent brown eyes and b blue eyes. We know that every human being begins life as a single cell, produced by the fusion of a female egg with a male sperm. Then each fertilised egg contains two units of the eye-colour gene (in addition to two of all other transmitted factors), that is, one unit from the sperm and one from the egg. Three combinations of eye-colour genes are, therefore, possible, BB, bb, and Bb.

The fertile cell divides in two, then four, eight, sixteen, and so on, until after many divisions and specialisations of cells into specific tissues, the adult is formed. Each comprises many millions and millions of cells, every one of which carries, for example, two exact copies of the eye-colour gene. Those with the gene pairs BB or Bb have brown eyes, and those with the bb genes have blue eyes. When both genes are present and the individual is brown-eyed, then the gene B is said to be dominant over the b, which is recessive. Such latent or recessive characteristics reappear in later generations in accordance with Mendel's laws.

Another phenomenon occurs in the heredity process: In the formation of the special germ cell (the egg cell of the mother and the sperm cell of the father) the number of genes in each is halved before fertilisation. This process is called meiosis. Thus a mother with gene pair, BB, will transmit gene B only; likewise, the mother with genes, bb, will transmit b only. But mothers with Bb combinations will produce both B and b egg cells in approximately equal numbers. Likewise for the father. If the dominant characteristic persists in both the sperm and the ovum, the offspring will be similar in the majority of cases. The recessive can result in 25 percent of cases.

Mendel did all his pioneer work in this field using garden peas as his basis. The laws he formulated are the basis of genetic science today.

How is the blueprint of our characteristics transmitted from generation to generation and from century to century with such accuracy? We have seen the basis by which the DNA replicates itself in chapter 9 and also an idea of the function played by proteins, enzymes, and amino acids in the structure of organisms. Let us now look at what happens to the nucleus of the cell when replication is in process.

Mitosis

Cells multiply by a process known as binary fission, during which cells grow and finally divide to produce two identical daughter cells. Division is preceded by the division of the nucleus in accordance with a remarkable series of events known collectively as mitosis.

In an undivided, or resting, cell, the nucleus appears as a spherical object surrounded by a nuclear membrane, devoid of structure except for certain bodies that can be picked out easily. These are known as nucleoli. At the onset of mitosis the nucleoli disappear and the nucleus concentrates into a number of thread-like structures known as chromosomes. Each of these threads thickens and splits longitudinally into two sister threads, which then arrange themselves in parallel. The threads then separate and migrate to the opposite side of the cell. A new nuclear membrane then forms around each of the two groups of threads or chromatids that uncoil and elongate and gradually disperse to form two identical resting nuclei. This process is followed by the division and separation of the entire cell. (See figure 11.)

Such an orderly process prompts the conclusion that only the mechanism of inheritance could demand such precision, when each cell is identical to its parent and sister. So mitosis ensures that each daughter cell possesses a complete set of chromosomes identical to the parent. It is by this process that plant cuttings can be propagated; likewise bacteria and other unicellular organisms can multiply. It is the genes, located on the chromosomes, that carry all the hereditary information necessary to ensure the specification of an entire organism.

If man were to reproduce his own kind by mitosis only, he would become two identical young men, both exactly alike. The two adults would divide into two and after a year or so would result in four identical men. The whole process would become a disaster, all identical men and no women on the planet!

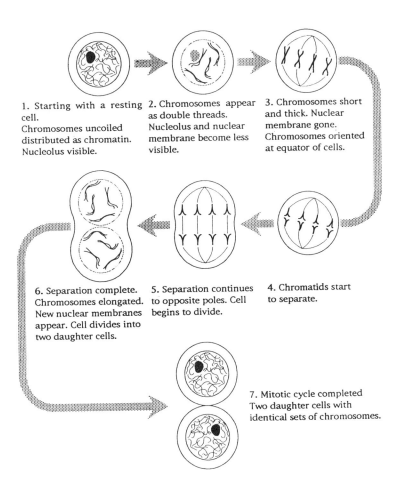

1. Starting with a resting cell. Chromosomes uncoiled distributed as chromatin. Nucleolus visible.

2. Chromosomes appear as double threads. Nucleolus and nuclear membrane become less visible.

3. Chromosomes short and thick. Nuclear membrane gone. Chromosomes oriented at equator of cells.

6. Separation complete. Chromosomes elongated. New nuclear membranes appear. Cell divides into two daughter cells.

5. Separation continues to opposite poles. Cell begins to divide.

4. Chromatids start to separate.

7. Mitotic cycle completed Two daughter cells with identical sets of chromosomes.

Figure 11. Cell division.

In fact when animals and plants reproduce, nature ensures that their offspring will not be identical except in the case of "identical twins." The reason for this brilliant variation from that of binary division is due to the process of meiosis. It applies to germ cells only.

While every cell of the body is subject to mitosis, germ cells (those involved in the reproduction only) are also subjected to the process of meiosis. Here the germ chromosomes do not split but separate into two groups, each with half the original number. Each group then forms the new nuclei; for this reason meiosis is sometimes referred to as "reduction division."

What force or electric field, however delicate, directs such processes? They are responsible for growth, maturity, succession, and transmission of characteristics.

A quantum leap of intellect is required if the source of energy that drives these billions of cells onwards in all their activities is to be understood. There are certainly many theories on the matter; none provide the answer.

The free energy reaching our planet has its origin in the nuclear fire within the core of the sun. The process gives rise to gamma radiation emitted from the surface of the sun. It is from this energy that all living organisms receive their supply. The need of energy for micro-organisms and living organisms is a fundamental requirement of life.

For life to begin, it is essential that a number of ingredients are present. A unique configuration of the cells is required subject to a suitable environment. The environment must ensure that all cells can communicate in an organised fashion and at the same time be subject to nuclear forces in harmony. These forces must form the "sparking plug"—the energy being supplied from the sun.

Life having begun, the specific organism synthesises food for survival. Specific chemical reactions are called for. They require energy-rich compounds. Nature provides these in the form of energy-rich units, viz. derivatives of phospheric acid and carboxylic acid. The most important of these are adenosine triphosphate (ATP) and creatinine phosphate. (See appendix 6.)

So energy from the sun penetrates the atmosphere, stimulates the mitochondria in cells, and initiates chemical activities leading to the formation of energy-rich compounds. These compounds power the cells and enable them to do their work. ATP, commonly referred to as the ''currency'' of energy metabolism in living cells, is uniquely designed for the role it plays in energy metabolism. But all this presupposes that the unique conditions for life must have already existed. The biochemical structure: proteins, enzymes, amino acids, and vitamins, must be in place, as indicated above.

Body Metabolism

In parallel with metabolism of individual cells there is the metabolism of the body as a whole. This takes a different pathway: heat and energy are produced by the breakdown of carbohydrate and noncarbohydrate sources to carbon dioxide and water, as indicated in figure 12.

Each and every step in metabolic processes is governed by a specific enzyme, which encourages the step for which the enzyme is designed. If the energy generated is not required immediately, it is stored in the form of high-energy molecules such as ATP and creatinine phosphate. It is used later. This metabolic process is, in essence, similar for most animals; certain details differ from species to species.

Many different substances are eaten each day as food; yet the process of digestion reduces the number of metabolic pathways to a few. The thousands of different proteins consumed by a human each day, for example, are reduced to a few amino acids. This process is governed by the number of effective enzymes available

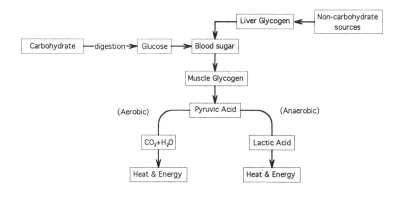

Figure 12. General metabolic pathway.

in each species. This, in turn, sets a limit to the number of pathways possible.

The human body is not equipped with the appropriate enzyme to digest some foods. Humans cannot, for example, digest grass because the enzyme necessary to break down grass is absent in the human makeup but present in oxen. There are thousands of examples of this phenomenon throughout the animal kingdom.

Metabolic Safety Valves

One might ask how this finely tuned metabolic process of the body reacts to overindulgence. The answer is that surplus protein, carbohydrate, or fat—and therefore amino acids—are deaminated in the liver and elsewhere and the nitrogen removed from the molecule. The remainder of the molecule, consisting of carbon, hydrogen, and oxygen, is dissipated as heat or energy.

All these ingenious chemical processes in metabolism are interchangeable: the body chemistry has the capacity to switch from one to another. It can switch from the breakdown of one dietary element to the building up of another less harmful or more desirable one, with ease. Directions for the initiation of such processes come from a battery of hormones and nervous telecommunications.

Chapter 14
Universal Laws

If there is one thing more than anything else that makes the universe unique, it is an insistence on order. Most of us go through life understanding little about the laws that govern the world around us; we take them all for granted. We give little thought as to why or how things happen—why light is as it is or proteins are constructed as they are. Yet it is on their stability that all our lives depend.

Let us look, briefly, at this order: The modern pictures of the universe date from 1924, when an American astronomer, Edwin Hubble, discovered that our galaxy is not the only one—there are millions of others. How did he achieve this? He noted that the apparent brightness of a star is dependent on two factors and only two: the amount of light the star radiates (luminosity) and its distance from us. Apparent brightness of a star equals quantity of light radiated relative to its distance from us.

The law works well for nearby stars, whose light can be seen. If any two terms in the above equation are known, the third can be calculated. By this method Hubble calculated the distance of nine galaxies. But most of the remainder are very much farther away, and only modern telescopes help us find them. There is another method of learning more about stars: the vast majority of them emit their own characteristic light spectrum, or ''finger-print.''

It is known, for example, that the relative brightness of the different colours in starlight corresponds to a specific frequency. The characteristics correspond exactly to the particular spectra of elements from which the light is emitted. This can readily be checked in a laboratory. So we can tell the star's temperature and distance from an examination of its light spectrum.

Moreover, certain colours are absent from the light of some stars. But, as stated above, every element has its own particular spectrum, so we can determine which elements are absent in a given star and which are present. We can even identify the star's "atmosphere." Light from stars tells us more; as a star recedes from us there is a red shift in its spectrum. The greater the shift towards the red end of the spectrum, the greater the velocity of recession. This is the Döppler effect applied to light. It operates as follows:

The frequency of light ranges from 4 to 700 million million waves per second. The different frequencies determine the different colours; the lowest frequency occurs at the red end of the spectrum. Should a source of light (a star) remain at a constant distance from us, the waves of light received from it would remain at a constant frequency. But suppose the light source is moving toward us. When the source emits the next wave crest, it will be nearer to us. The time required for each wave crest to reach us will be less than if the source were stationary. Likewise an increase in time is required by each wave crest when the source is travelling away from us.

By this method Hubble showed in 1929 that the universe is expanding in every direction and that the farther out the galaxies have travelled the faster they move. Is the universe, then, expanding faster than the critical velocity when gravity is no longer able to contain the expansion? All the evidence points to the fact that this is not so; the expansion is slowing down. (The matter will be referred to in more detail in chapter 18.)

It was an American physicist, of Russian background, Alexander Friedman, who identified the expanding aspect of the cosmos. He made two assumptions: (1) the universe looks the same in whatever direction we look at it, and (2) this fact would be true if we observed the universe from any other location. Friedman had predicted the phenomenon two years before Hubble proved it in 1929.

If the universe is expanding in such a manner and the galaxies are hurtling themselves farther and farther apart, like dots painted on the surface of a balloon which is being inflated, they must have originated at some common point, which would have been extremely dense.

In 1965 two American physicists, Arno Penzias and Robert Wilson, working for the Bell Telephone laboratory, were testing a highly sensitive microwave detector. (Microwaves are similar to light waves, but with a very much lower frequency.) Having carefully developed this detector, they found it was picking up far more noise than they had expected. Wherever they pointed the detector disc, vertically or horizontally, day or night, summer or winter, the noise did not diminish. It was then realised that this noise was coming from outside the solar system and from far beyond our galaxy—from across the entire observable universe. We now know that this noise does not vary. Penzias and Wilson had stumbled upon the remnants of the searing heat George Gamow had suggested years previously was the origin of the universe. Such were the events that led to the discovery of the big bang theory, now accepted as the correct explanation for the origin of the universe by most leading scientists.

A general characteristic of matter is that it is vulnerable to temperature. The higher the energy, the higher the temperature and the less structured order in subatomic matter itself. The identity of matter undergoes a uniform fade-out with increase in temperature; solids become liquid, then gas, then plasma, in which even atoms lose their structure and become dissociated from electrons and ions. At higher temperatures the nuclei of atoms break up. It is evident that this was the state of cosmological material at about one second after the big bang. It consisted of a mixture of protons, neutrons, and electrons. Prior to that instant (before 10^{-6} second) the temperature and density of nuclear particles (protons and neutrons) were so high that their identity was lost. Cosmological material was reduced to "a soup of quarks," the contents of protons.

The philosopher Parmenides, who lived in 1500 B.C., was the first, as far as we know, to shout from the rooftops, "Nothing can come out of nothing!" Many philosophers have since come to accept his dictum. But there is still a problem. Scientists have no idea as to the ultimate origin of the big bang; how can the universe have come into being from "nothing" without violating the laws of physics? But the laws of physics are only those known to us, or within our finite understanding. While physics has made enormous strides since the times of Galileo and Newton, it is impossible to set a limit to its boundaries or determine all the laws governing the universe as a whole.

As stated in page 17 it was thought that hot bodies dissipate energy in the form of electromagnetic radiation at a uniform rate, irrespective of the frequency of waves. In 1900 Max Planck realised that there was something odd about such an assumption: How could energy be radiated uniformly at all frequencies? How could a hot body radiate the same amount of energy with a frequency of 1 million million waves per second at one instant and 5 million million waves per second at another? He reasoned that varying the frequency from zero to infinity implied that the total energy radiated would be infinite, which was impossible. Planck arrived at the conclusion that electromagnetic radiation took place in bursts, or "quanta," and each quantum possessed a specific amount of energy, which increased with frequency.

In 1905 Einstein suggested that the characteristics of photo-electricity could be explained readily by applying Planck's quantum theory. Photoelectricity is described as that phenomenon whereby electrons on the surface atoms of a metal become energised and jump clear of the metal when light is shone on them. Light of high frequency, such as ultraviolet light, has more effect than light of low frequency. This is the basis of the photoelectric cell in common use today. The theory subsequently confirmed that light consisted of particles, called photons, or waves. It was the frequency of the wave or proton that had real power.

The quantum hypothesis of Max Planck set a new train of thought in motion. Einstein readily accepted the concept and developed the photoelectric effect, but in 1926 another German scientist, Werner Heisenberg, who had formulated his famous "uncertainty" principle, said: "In order to predict the future position and velocity of a particle, one has to measure its present position and velocity accessibility."

The obvious way to achieve this is by shining light on the particle in motion. The particle will scatter some of the photons of light, and this will indicate the particle's position. The accurate position of the particle is dependent on the wavelength of the light used, that is, the distance between two successive wave crests. For greater accuracy we must use light of shorter wavelength. But as shown by Planck, one cannot use an arbitrarily small amount of light—less than one quantum is not possible. A quantum of light of very high frequency will certainly disturb the particle and alter its velocity in an uncertain way. In other words, the more accurately one tries to measure the position of the particle, the less accurately one can measure its velocity, and vice versa. Heisenberg showed that one cannot know where an atom or electron or whatever is located and know how it is moving at one and the same time. He showed this to be a fundamental property of matter. It is the principle of uncertainty. He said: "By getting to smaller and smaller units, we do not come to fundamental units, or indivisible units, but we *do* come to a point where division has no meaning."

Chapter 15
Quantum Mechanics

Quantum physics was developed in the 1920s. The concept was initiated by Max Planck when he began to think of energy in terms of lumps or quanta. The concept was further developed by others such as Albert Einstein, Niels Bohr, Werner Heisenberg, Erwin Schrödinger, Max Born, Max Jordan, and Paul Dirac. Heisenberg's uncertainty principles played an important role in its development. He showed that one can be certain of nothing when dealing with the microworld. We now know that we cannot be sure of the behaviour of an atom, much less an electron; a strange and mysterious world exists where common sense has no place.

Each decade brings new discoveries in relation to the paradox of knowledge. With each year advances are made in devising better instruments with which to observe nature. The frontiers of scientific knowledge are being pushed further back with debate, discussion, and argument. This is the seedbed of learning.

The ancient university town of Göttingen, 170 miles southwest of Berlin, was the centre of much activity between the two world wars. The place was a backwater where scholars gathered to associate with distinguished professors. It was here in 1800 that Karl Friedrich Gauss showed that when an observer looks, for example, at a star, he knows there is a multitude of causes for error. By taking several readings he hopes that the best estimate of the star's position will be the average—the centre of scatter.

Gauss went further and asked what the scatter of the errors revealed. Thus he developed his famous Gaussian curve. Subsequently he become quite intolerant of philosophers who claimed that "they had a road to knowledge more perfect than that of observation." He became quite odd and eccentric.

It was here too that Max Born was appointed to the chair of theoretical physics in 1924 but was dismissed by Hitler in 1933. Max Born had the remarkable gift of drawing brilliant men around him and getting the best from them. Göttingen became the centre where science was dominated by relativity, where many scholars such as Werner Heisenberg, Hans Krebs, and Joseph John Thompson were active. It was here that theories in quantum mechanics flourished and put an end to important principles of classical mechanics—that of the mechanistic reductionist philosophy—replacing it with abstract vision. The quantum characteristics of electromagnetic radiation (light) together with the uncertainty principle formed its basis. The Newtonian concept was replaced with a mathematical one involving wave functions as a statistical approach. But wave functions are only a convenient mathematical device for handling statistics.

Böhr's theory of the atom accounted for many aspects of atomic phenomena, yet it had limitations. It could not explain, for example, why some of the lines of the spectroscope were more intense than others; nor could it account for the fact that many spectral lines are made up of several independent lines of different wavelengths. An appeal to atomic behaviour was required. It was supplied in 1926 with quantum physics.

The essential differences between Newtonian mechanics and quantum mechanics lie in what each *describes*. In Newtonian mechanics the future history of a particle is completely determined by its initial position and velocity, together with the forces that act on it. Quantum mechanics also arrives at relationships between observable quantities. But the uncertainty principle insists that the nature of an observable quantity is quite different when one is dealing with the subatomic world.

Cause and effect remain related, but what they convey needs interpretation. In quantum mechanics the kind of certainty about the future proposed by Newtonian mechanics is impossible, because the initial position and velocity of a particle cannot be established accurately, as explained earlier. The future is unknowable because the present is unknowable.

The quantities that quantum mechanics explores are *probabilities.* Instead of claiming, for example, that the radius of the electron's orbit of a hydrogen atom in the ground, or normal, state is always exactly 5.3×10^{-11}m, quantum mechanics states that that is the most *probable* radius. If a suitable experiment is conducted, trial results will yield different values, either larger or smaller, but the value most likely to be found will be 5.3×10^{-11}m.

Dirac, Böhr, and Schrödinger showed that "Newtonian mechanics is nothing but an approximate version of quantum mechanics." The certainties proclaimed by Newtonian mechanics are entirely illusory. So we are back to uncertainty. Microscopic bodies consist of so many individual atoms that departure from average behaviour goes unnoticed.

As stated in page 45, de Broglie showed that electrons orbit the nucleus not in concentric circles, but in "wavy paths." (See figure 5.) The more energy that is imparted to the atom, the more "waves" the electron makes on its way round that "wavy orbit," releasing energy at each crest and absorbing energy at each trough. One can see, immediately, that this phenomenon of nature is complex and, for any given instant, has a specific meaning.

We are therefore faced with the reality that if the electron is to have position or momentum, depending on which aspect is of interest to us, then these two parameters are inseparable from the actual measuring apparatus and, indeed, the actual observer who is doing the observing. What a strange situation! *The observer and the observed become related* in a strange way. But the macroworld of everyday objects such as cars, boats, houses, etc., is made up of the microworld; so, too, are the measuring apparatus and the experimenters. Paul Davies put it well: "The macro world needs the micro world to constitute it and the micro world needs the macro world to define it."

Notwithstanding this, there is a deep suspicion associated with quantum mechanics by many. It is the physics that does not concern itself with the rules of clockwork—it rejects them. When it comes to atoms, quantum mechanics comes into its own, using rules that are those of roulette.

The ability of quantum particles to possess incompatibility, or contradictory properties, such as being both wave and particle, prompted Niels Böhr to introduce his theory of "complementarity." He recognised that it is not paradoxical for an electron to be both wave and particle, because both aspects are never displayed in a contradictory way at the same time. He believed that "the incompatibilities of being both wave and particle are not contradictory. They are quite complementary: it depends on which experiment one is carrying out and which piece of information one is looking for. In other words, the answer depends on the observer."

All this demands a reappraisal of the nature of reality. It leaves us with new "truths" with which we must come to terms. Some would question whether an electron is a "thing" or a "mental concept" or a ghost; all the evidence now is that it is "matter" with strange properties that have purpose. In the overall context, it is not easily understood.

The work of Erwin Schrödinger showed that quantum mechanics is a practical branch of physics and has been extremely successful. Its application has given the world the laser, the transistor, microelectronics, electron microscopes, nuclear power, and much more. He defined the system as best he could in mathematical terms (the Schrödinger equation*). His work again confirmed that as soon as a measurement is taken, or a system is observed, the deterministic aspect is destroyed; the system (or the particle) no longer obeys the normal microworld regime. One of two possibilities therefore arises: change occurs to the particle in its orbit either when nobody is looking or when the particle is subjected to a stream of photons. The effects are unknown. It all seems like searching for a needle in a haystack. The needle is there; it is a matter of where one looks for it.

This phenomenon gave rise to a famous debate between Böhr and Einstein in the 1920s. Böhr accepted that atomic uncertainty is intrinsic to nature. He believed that familiar objects, such as snooker balls, comply with clockwork rules and atoms comply with the rules of roulette. Einstein disagreed. He claimed that "God does not play dice"; if an atom existed as an independent entity, then at the very least it should have location and motion. Einstein could not accept the tacit implication that the atom had a ghostlike and mysterious property.

The debate raged for years. Experiments were devised by many to prove who was right and who was wrong. It was left to Alain Aspect of the University of Paris to finally resolve the problem in 1982 with an elegant experiment, the results of which are now accepted.

Einstein had devised an experiment in 1931 that he hoped would expose the fraud of quantum ghosts and show that every event had a cause. His experiment was based on the principle

---

*Schrödinger's equation cannot be derived from "first principles" but represents a first principle itself. All we can do is postulate Schrödinger's equation, solve it for a variety of physical conditions, and compare the results of the calculations with the results of experiments. If they agree, the postulate embodied in his equation is valid; if not, the postulate must be discarded and another approach explored.

that the various ghost particles referred to do not act independently, but as one. He based his experiment on the principle that if a particle is made to explode and the two halves (A and B) fly apart, the two should behave in an exactly similar manner, except that particle A will spin clockwise while particle B will spin counter clockwise, no matter how far they move apart, by Newton's third law. Einstein's experiment could not be carried out in practice.

Alaine Aspect, while using the same principle, employed two photons (ghosts) of light as the experimental fragments. They were emitted simultaneously by an atom. Two polarised screens (which will allow light to vibrate in one plane only) were placed one on each side of the source of the photons (or ghosts) and equidistanced from that source. (See figure 13.) The polarising screens filter out the ghost photons, which do not align their vibrations to correspond with the axis of the screen. Thus only ghost photons with the correct orientation will get through.

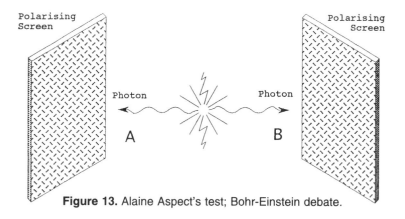

Figure 13. Alaine Aspect's test; Bohr-Einstein debate.

In the experiment, ghost photons A and B operated because of their similar action and reaction to one another. If photon A was blocked, so also was photon B. But when the polarised screens were oriented a little obliquely to one another, cooperation diminished, as polarisation of the ghost photons could not align correctly. Einstein's theory was thus proved wrong!

Isn't there a strangeness about the subatomic world? Let us accept it for what it is and learn from it.

*   *   *

All materials are radioactive to a greater or lesser extent. The higher the atomic number of an element, the more radioactivity it displays. Very heavy elements are extremely unstable and constantly give up electrons and protons to achieve stability in themselves. (See figure 14.)

In doing so they give rise to lighter and more stable elements lower down the periodic table. This is another example of Mother Nature's ingenious tricks.

No single phenomenon has played so significant a role in the development of nuclear physics as radioactivity. An unstable nucleus will decay in order to achieve a new configuration that is stable or will lead to one that will be.

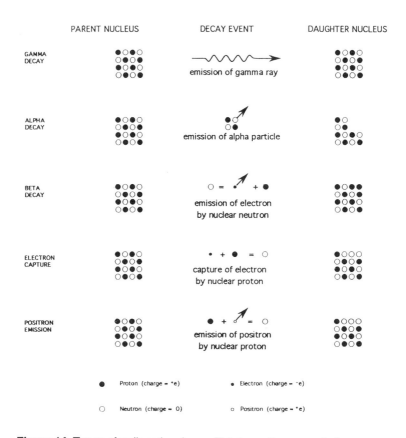

Figure 14. Types of radioactive decay. This is another aspect of quantum physics. The forces that influence this phenomenon are not understood. The fact that we do not understand them is no justification for claiming that "cause and effect" is violated. All the indications are that in the near future scientific developments will have made the necessary strides to enable us to understand the cause.

106

Chapter 16
Cause and Effect

From earliest times it was believed that the universe had a cause and that cause was God. Plato and Aristotle were of a similar view; so also were Saint Augustine and Saint Thomas Aquinas. More recently Gottfried von Leibniz and Samuel Clarke employed the reasoning as an argument for the existence of God. But Immanuel Kant and Bertrand Russell consistently rejected it. I will refer to the matter further in chapter 20.

One of the most important developments in scientific thinking since the beginning of time was Einstein's development of the equation $E = mc^2$ where E represents energy, m=mass of particle, and c= speed of light (300,000 kilometres per second). In one fell swoop Einstein tied together (correctly, as proved later) energy, mass, and the velocity of light. Using this equation he showed that nothing can travel faster than light. (See appendix 1.) Subsequent research, using particle accelerators, showed that theory to be correct. We have already seen that a particle increases in mass as it approaches the speed of light. Some scientists claimed that this represents an example of the "creation of matter out of nothing," but this is not tenable, as the phenomenon is directly related to energy input. Einstein had shown that matter is nothing more than "frozen energy."

Can matter, then, be created or destroyed by natural means? Scientists prior to the twentieth century believed that it could not be—they were inclined to the belief that the universe was of infinite age and "what was here was made to stay." Paul Dirac, however, wondered what would happen if one could unlock matter and allow it to return to energy. After all, matter and energy are made up of a collection of atoms, and atomic particles comply with the laws of quantum mechanics. There must be a relationship, he thought, between quantum mechanisms and relativity, even though Einstein never accepted quantum mechanics. Einstein considered the claim "spooky," having something of the three-card-trick quality.

Despite the accuracy with which quantum mechanics accounts for many properties relating to the hydrogen atom, it was unable to provide a complete description of the atom unless the phenomena of "electron spin" and the "exclusion principle" were also taken into account. It was George Uhlenbeck and Sam Goudsmit who proposed the former in 1925 and Wolfgang Pauli who proposed the latter; the three were successful.

The increase in mass of a particle with velocity, together with the baffling property of angular momentum, led Dirac in 1930 to investigate the possibility of the existence of completely new particles. His celebrated mathematical analysis of the subject led him to the conclusion that two distinct types of electrons exist—one with a positive charge and one with a negative. He called these "matter" and "antimatter." Carl Anderson confirmed Dirac's finding in 1933.

The work of Dirac and Anderson subsequently resulted in the reproduction of matter with high-energy acceleration. Particles so reproduced had both positive and negative charges. In this way it was possible to "re-create" electrons and antielectrons, protons and antiprotons, and numerous other particles, provided an abundance of energy is available in the first instance.

As a result it became fashionable amongst some physicists to believe that man was now able to "create matter out of nothing" and therefore explain away the theory of the steady-state universe. It was even claimed that the whole of matter contains exactly equal quantities of matter and antimatter. If this were so, the opposing charges would automatically annihilate one another should they come in contact. This would result in all matter being annihilated. But such does not happen; the universe remains very much intact. Many reasons are put forward to explain away the phenomenon, but all of them consist of nothing more than guesswork at best. The most plausible of these is that the reproduction of matter and antimatter in the laboratory is never symmetrical (with an equal quantity of each). Such conditions at the time of the big bang would have been most improbable, as different types of particles would naturally emerge at different stages of cooling after the initial explosion.

Should there have been an imbalance between matter and antimatter at the time of the big bang, or shortly afterwards, the heat generated in the annihilation process would add to the enormous background radiation left over after the big bang itself. A number of scientists have endeavoured to check the quantity of ''leftover'' background heat. They all found that the results made surprisingly good sense.

The processes thus described do not represent ''the creation of matter from nothing,'' as claimed, but the conversion of preexisting energy from one form to another or from one fundamental particle to another. An unimaginably large quantity of such energy appeared some 18 billion years ago. Only a small portion of it has been accounted for.

As stated earlier, one achievement of the twentieth century was the discovery that heat is energy and energy is matter; all three are concealed in a form related to the velocity of electromagnetic radiation. We now know that if we have enough of one, we can, with suitable equipment, convert to either of the remaining two. This phenomenon is, in a strange way, something similar to the manner in which protein, carbohydrates, and fat can be converted one to the other in animals.

Chapter 17
Intellect, Order, and Free Will

The average weight of the adult male human brain is 1,380 grams; that of the female is 1,250 grams. The adult body supporting the brain is about fifty times heavier. At birth, the body is almost an appendage to its brain, since it is only two or three times heavier. The brain is described as the cerebral hemisphere, and all its surface is covered with grey matter (cells of the cerebral cortex). It is formed of a number of separate departments, all interlinked and the whole consisting of well over 100 billion neurons, or nerve cells, capable of conveying impulses to stimulate nerve centres.

It is not proposed to discuss the anatomy of the brain, accepted as the most complex and most ingenious machine ever devised. It is now believed that the information content necessary for its evolution exceeds anything imagined by humankind. Discussion of the subject, therefore, must include the world of behaviour, consciousness, thought, creativity, free will, and dreams, a world where the subjective and the objective are related. It is a sobering thought that every man-made object on this planet has been the product of that brain; so also for every species of cultivated plant or animal. The physiological functions of the brain are myriad; its inventive and creative powers transcend everything else known.

Man possesses an emotional content of profound dimensions. He has within him a deep-seated faith in a higher Being. It is manifested in the most primitive of men. All thoughts, emotion, feelings, and intuitions are centred in the brain. Whether he admits it or not, man is frequently in communication with forces that he cannot see. To delve into these forces is the rub, the challenge, the mystery.

Extensive research has been taking place at various centres throughout the world in the past fifteen years in an endeavour to find out how the brain works. Stephen Rose, professor of neurophysiology at the Open University, Milton Keynes, England, in his book *The Making of Memory* confirms that it is extremely difficult to unlock the secrets of biological memory. Rose and his colleagues believe that if we could find out how memory works we would then have some means of deciphering the most important link between brain and behaviour.

Learning processes have been studied using young birds, slugs, and worms in an endeavour to determine the cellular changes that occur in the brain resulting from external stimuli. These changes have been measured microscopically. They are known to be caused by chemical processes that produce signals between nerve cells in particular areas of the brain. The signals, in turn, give rise to the production of particular proteins, which return to the signalling points between cells, causing the cell structure to change. It is believed that this process simulates ''learning,'' but how the learning process is actually stored (memory) is not known. It is known that the memory process involves wiring diagrams linking millions of nerve cells; but this involves atomic activity, which indicates that the quantum factor (the uncertainty principle) is involved in an unexpected way.

It is one thing to study the circuit diagram of a simple washing machine, which may have as many as twenty electronic components—it is not always obvious from the diagram how the components interact to make the washing machine work. Imagine doing the same for a chick's brain, which has the equivalent of billions of components. How about the human brain?

A discussion on the mind is an intellectual exercise—the dominance of mind over matter. The word *mind,* in this context, is not dissociated from the brain—it is the software, in computer language. The mind is one's own consciousness, experience, self; it is the soul for those who consciously commune with a Higher Order.

Should one listen to a Beethoven symphony, for example, it is not the individual notes played by individual orchestral instruments that are Beethoven; it is the overall poignancy, drama, and beauty of the integrated work. No particular phrase in the symphony is complete; the whole movement is.

The brain may be viewed at two levels: a lower level that relates to the workings of individual cells through electrophysical connections and a higher level that relates to elaborate electrical systems that move in patterns. The latter might be considered analogous to a series of parallel ''canals'' filled with information rather than water. From each canal, volumes of specific knowledge can be drawn at will and integrated with the contents of other ''canals'' to form concepts. Should the banks of the ''canals'' overflow, mental confusion ensues.

A creative artist may suddenly change his mind as to the way a melody should run or the way a figure on a canvas should take shape. We are, because of our mental makeup, of an indeterministic nature. We are not governed by the laws of Newtonian mechanics, where everything proceeds like clockwork; there is an indeterministic element.

It is said that the activities of a person are determined by his personality; what does this mean? Determinism hardly implies that events occur in spite of our action; many occur because we determine them. Professor D. M. McKay, a specialist in the field of neurology, believes that complete self-predictability is impossible. This makes sense if Heisenberg's uncertainty principle applies to the cells of the brain. As stated earlier, if we could predict the behaviour of the atoms forming brain cells at any given instant, we could predict the future. But the theory of uncertainty prohibits this; we therefore have free will. The quantum factor emerges once more.

The relationship between free will and responsibility for crime, for example, is often the subject of controversy. If free will is illusory, why should anybody be blamed for his misdeeds? If everything is predetermined, predestined, or preordained, we are caught in a deadly trap set in advance of our existence. Some scientists introduce God at this juncture in a fashion that complicates the picture. They ask: "If God is omnipotent, why does He not prevent evil? If the evil in the world is also God's plan, then He is not benevolent; if the evil is contrary to His intention, then He is not omnipotent." Professor Paul Davies asked: "Must we therefore conclude that evil (in perhaps a limited amount) is all part of God's plan? Or is God not free after all to prevent us from acting against Him?"

Clearly the quantum factor undermines determinism and ensures that we have free will. Granted, we may frequently run up against that which "puzzles the will and makes us bear the ills we have rather than fly to those we know not of."

With regard to God's function in the affair, it is clear that the universe has been designed and is relatively simple, while we are complex; it is also clear that science is possible only because we live in an ordered universe, which complies with simple mathematical rules; that evolution is a fact and evolves in distinct jumps in time separated by large plateaus (contrary to Darwin's theory); that heredity is based on genetic codes of an incomprehensible uniqueness; that space-time is elastic; and that the basis of the universe is founded on four fundamental forces. As to whether we are unique on this planet, we will refer to this in the next chapter.

It used to be standard practice to reduce all physical processes to the laws of Newtonian mechanics, that is, to say all processes are reduced to the behaviour of particles with respect to their location and velocity. As we have seen, this is the philosophy of reductionism. But such philosophy is gone; the new physics has undermined it foundations.

Professor Paul Davies puts it well: ''Complete reductionism is nothing more than a vague promise founded on the outdated and now discredited concept of determinism. By ignoring the significance of higher levels in nature, complete reductionism simply dodges many of the questions about the world that interest us.''

But for the fact that order prevails it would be impossible to make a scientific study of anything; any mathematical analysis would be impossible. Kant claimed that the human mind imposed order on the world so as to make sense of it. But in the absence of a knowledge of atomic physics or the evolution of galaxies, stars, or atomic elements, no one could take Kant's statement seriously. It is significant that the protagonists of the steady-state theory, or the philosophy of determinism as a whole, come from amongst philosophers devoid of knowledge of quantum physics, relativity, or radioactivity.

Everywhere we look, from the distant galaxies to the internal workings of the atom, we find organisation. Energy and matter are not distributed at random; on the contrary, they have a hierarchical distribution: atoms, molecules, crystals, life, planets, stars, and galaxies. Organisation takes many guises: regularity of the solar system, ocean waves and currents, behaviour of molecules in a gas, the complex nature of living creatures, ability of the organic to recover after injury, genetics, the migratory instincts of birds, photosynthesis. Examples are numerous.

The elegance of atomic harmony is cast into stark relief when we consider that the force that binds the electron to the proton is mathematically simple. Atoms could not exist but for the fact that the attraction of the electron for the proton is an inverse square law. That is to say if the separation between the proton and electron is doubled, the force reduces to one-quarter of its value; if the separation distance is trebled, the force is one-ninth. It is ingenious.

In the design of atoms there is another order: How are the internal nuclear particles held together? How are protons, positively charged, held together? Gravity is far too weak, and electric forces are repulsive between like charges. There must exist a strong attraction force to bind protons in the nucleus. Tests have shown that this force does exist and is stronger than electricity and disappears rapidly at a distance close to the surface of the protons in question. It is called the strong nuclear force and does not obey the simple inverse square law. It is now known that in the subatomic domain quantum effects are extremely important. Again the central feature of quantum effect is that energy is transmitted in discrete lumps.

When physicists found that they could get the nucleus of an atom to yield at least some of its content using accelerators, dozens of new and hitherto unsuspected particles appeared. For a while the number and variety of particles released from proton bashing were bewildering, but gradually a pattern of symmetry emerged. Families of particles made their appearance. So much so that Yuval Ne'eman and Murray Gell-Mann became fascinated with the whole subtle elegance that their symmetries displayed. Families containing eight, ten, and more particles have recently made their appearance; more are apparently on the way. Where do the numbers stop? Appendix 7, Table B gives an indication of position.

It does not take exceptional powers of vision to see that there is a distinct unfolding of organised complexity within nature. Paul Davies states:

I have been at pains to argue that the steady unfolding of organised complexity in the universe is a fundamental property of nature ... important attempts have been made to model complex structures and processes in physics, chemistry, biology, astronomy and ecology. We have seen how spontaneous self-organisation tends to occur in far-from-equilibrium open non-linear systems with a high degree of feedback. Such systems, far from being universal, are actually the norm in nature. By contrast the closed linear systems studied in traditional mechanics, or the equilibrium systems of standard thermodynamics, are idealisations of a very special sort.

For decades there has been a tendency for some physicists to discard processes or systems in nature that they did not understand. This is less than intellectual honesty. We have only to look at the four fundamental forces of nature to realise how little we know about universal laws. The atomic structure is continuing to reveal more and more.

It is clear that higher and lower orders of creativity exist. The increase in chaos and creativity has an intrinsic uniformity; unique leaps forward from lower to higher orders, independent of what went before, are measures that puzzle the will. Karl Popper said:

Today some of us have learned to use the word "evolution" differently. For we think that evolution—the evolution of the universe, and especially the evolution of life on earth—has produced new things; real novelty .... The story of evolution suggests that the universe has never ceased to be creative, or inventive.

K. Denbeigh is of a similar opinion:

Let us ask: can genuinely new things come into existence during the course of time; things, that is to say, which are not entailed by the properties of other things which existed previously?

Isaac Newton said:

Whence arises all that order and beauty we see in the world?

It is true that designs of a complex order can sometimes be explained away in terms of perfectly ordinary processes. We must therefore be cautious of inferring the existence of a designer when we meet something that looks complicated. There are many other phenomena for which we have no known laws to assist us: We are unable to define life; we do not know why the atoms of the elements are constructed as they are; we have no idea exactly how stars are formed or what decides their mass. Also, we know little or nothing about the storage of inventive or creative capacity in the brain. Computers are merely followers.

Chapter 18
Are We Unique?

In previous chapters there were occasions to refer to coincidences in nature, but there are cosmic coincidences that extend far beyond planetary considerations and scientific knowledge. Let us look at some.

It takes a few billion years for a galaxy to form and for its first stars to process hydrogen and helium and then continue to form the heavier elements, such as carbon, oxygen, etc. These stars eventually wear themselves out and die in a blaze of glory, flinging their precious contents far and wide. New stars and associated planets form from the debris of the deceased stars; life may evolve on some of their associated planets. For all this to happen and for man to arrive and wonder what its all about, the age of the universe must be in the order of 16 to 20 billion years and, it is therefore about 16 to 20 billion light-years across. Figure 15 indicates the order of the stellar cycle.

The fact that we are carbon-based confirms that the universe is of minimum size and minimum age. Some argue that the universe cannot possibly have been designed to produce carbon-based intelligence solely for a single planet orbiting a tiny star. They claim that the machinery forming the universe is far too large, too ingenious, and too complicated for one single purpose. But if the laws of physics and chemistry have not been altered, then this argument falls down.

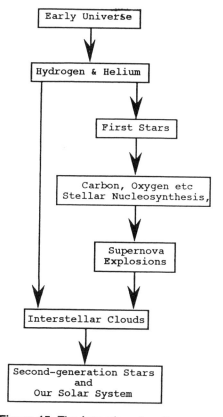

Figure 15. The formation of matter.

It is an extraordinary fact that the universe happens to have been expanding since the big bang at just the correct rate to allow galaxies, stars, and planets to form. Is it equally coincidental that the aeons of time involved in the process of expansion also correspond to the time required for carbon formation and carbon-based life?

Moreover, oxygen and carbon atoms are about equally common in living matter, just as they are in the universe at large.

While it is possible to imagine life in a universe with a moderate imbalance between oxygen and carbon, a large imbalance would forbid its existence. A greater excess of carbon would prevent the formation of many materials on which life is dependent (rock and soil, for example). Excess of oxygen would simply burn up any carbon-based biochemicals that existed. This unique balance between oxygen and carbon is dependent on the origin of the chemical elements generated inside stars.

Hydrogen and helium can evolve out of pure energy, that which resulted from the big bang; but the reason both elements are converted to heavier elements inside stars is because heavier elements are more suitable for storage. The transformation process requires nuclear fusion which occurs within stars. Because four atoms of hydrogen have a mass greater than the mass of one atom of helium, it followed that A. S. Eddington's proposed transformation *would* yield energy. His proposal proved absolutely correct:

$$H \longrightarrow 4He + Energy$$

There is another consideration equally inexplicable but nevertheless a fact: our knowledge of the geography of the universe is limited to the distribution of galaxies across the sky. The total mass of all these galaxies has been estimated (using the Doppler shift). If we know the rate at which the galaxies are moving apart, the total mass required to stop them (gravity) from getting out of control can be calculated to within reasonable limits of accuracy. This calculation has been done many times, and it is found that the total mass of *all* galaxies is only one-tenth the mass required to keep them gravity-bound, that is, the critical mass. It is now known that the other 90 percent of the mass required is concealed in the form of "dark stuff" (or matter), which appears to be uniformly distributed throughout the universe.

It is this "material" that has controlled the rate of expansion of the universe from the beginning and gave stars sufficient time to adequately cook their ingredients before they blew up. The content, extent, and location of this "stuff" are not known; the indications are that its existence gives critical mass to an orderly expansion of the universe.

It is possible to get an indication how much of this "stuff" is needed for gravitational purposes to bring the expansion of the universe to a halt; the total density of the universe is estimated to be approximately three atoms per cubic metre at present. Long ago, it was more dense; in time to come it will be much less dense. On this matter John Gribbon and Martin Rees are of the opinion:

> When we convert the discussion with the proper description of the Universe, Einstein's mathematical descriptions of space and time and work backwards to see how critical the expansion rate must have been at the time of the Big Bang, we find that the universe is balanced far more crucially than the metaphorical knife edge . . . If we push back to the earliest time at which our theories of physics can be thought to have any validity, the implication is that the relevant number, the so-called "density parameter," was set, in the beginning, with an accuracy of 1 part in 10^{60}. Changing that parameter, either way, by a fraction given by a decimal point followed by 60 zeros and a 1 would have made the universe unsuitable for life as we know it.

It does seem an extraordinary fluke that gravity has so finely tuned the rate of expansion of the universe to enable building, burning, and death of stars to take place at a rate that ensures our survival. The fluke is so exceptional, bearing in mind the vast periods of time involved, that the other cosmic coincidences (speed of light, quantum effects, Planck's constant, the charge on a proton, universal gravity, the electric force binding protons, colour force binding quarks) must be taken in perspective.

Since light from very distant galaxies has spent several billion years reaching us, it can reveal how fast the universe was expanding in the remote past. By comparing the velocities of recession of very distant galaxies with those of nearby galaxies, cosmologists can calculate how quickly the expansion is decelerating and so deduce whether it will eventually stop expanding or reverse itself. They find that the universe is, to all intents and purposes, "flat," that is to say, that it will never either expand nor contract. The coincidence of this phenomenon has been a source of worry to many cosmologists. They find it incredible that the big bang should have created such incomprehensible quantities of energy (matter) to enable some to form into stars and some to remain as "dark stuff" and assist gravity. It has also been suggested that this "dark stuff" does not necessarily have to be ordinary matter similar to that of stars, the Earth, or ourselves, that is, protons and neutrons. Nature has not yielded up all her secrets with respect to fundamental particles—accelerators or no accelerators.

It is a sobering thought that this universe contains approximately a billion billion (10^{18}) stars. At least 1 percent of that number (10 million billion [10^6]) should be reasonably similar to our sun, which is just an average star.

If we now guess half of 1 percent of that number possess planetary systems similar to ours, we would have 50,000 billion (5×10^{10}) of them something like our own. Such numbers make our home unimaginably small. But could it be that these billions of (hypothetical) homes exist purely to ensure that our simple life-supporting home might survive?

Notwithstanding such cosmic coincidences as the controlled rate of expansion of the universe, the necessity for "dark stuff" to make up the shortfall, and the capacity of gravity to have an infinite range of action, there is that other force—the electric force. This strange force more than compensates for the "shortcomings" in the strength of gravity at close range. It is millions

Chapter 19

Integration of the Whole

previous chapters indicated that certain physical laws and
ants of nature play a vital role in governing the universe:
r forces govern the structure of nuclei; electromagnetic
govern charged materials; gravity governs the size and
e of stars; the velocity of light relates energy and mass;
tivity governs the stability of the elements; DNA directs
nce; differences in people are governed by cell division;
ability of organisms to be self-generating and self-or-
is complementary to all of these processes. There are
s of other examples that manifest the uniqueness of na-
rvive, organise, and self-create.

s been shown that the sizes of galaxies, stars, planets,
oms, etc., are related and are the consequence of the
f the fundamental forces and the natural constants re-
eviously. Gribbin and Rees in their book *The Stuff of*
e point out that some kind of cosmic rule must govern
alaxies, as well as the size of ourselves. Some indica-
is provided when we plot a graph showing how the
known object is related to its size. (See figure 16.)

were no connection governing the size of such ob
e points on the graph would be scattered. But th
plots lie on a uniform curve gives a clue to wh
An examination of figure 16 shows that the line A
iverse into two distinct regions.

of times stronger than gravity within the confines of the nucleus of atoms. It binds protons together. Outside the nucleus this electric force fades rapidly.

Again, spectroscopic studies of light from the oldest stars show no trace of heavier elements other than those that emerged from the big bang. In the 1950s it became evident that the universe is essentially composed of two primary elements: hydrogen, 75 percent and helium, 25 percent. Astrophysicists have constructed models showing how these two elements formed protons and neutrons in the first milliseconds of cooling after the "bang." The question is how the essential molecules of life, carbon, oxygen, nitrogen, and phosphorus came about. It didn't take long for astrophysicists to guess the trick by which such a marvellous process was achieved in the case of carbon, oxygen, etc. It involves the successful sticking together of helium nuclei. The process operates as follows: Helium-4 contains two protons and two neutrons. This is a stable configuration. Atoms that are made up of whole numbers of helium-4 nuclei are very stable and very common. Moreover, carbon, which contains twelve nucleons, and oxygen, which contains sixteen, are also stable elements. They are essential to life. How are they formed?

In 1952 Edward Salpeter suggested that carbon 12 might be produced in a rapid two-step process in which two alpha particles (helium nuclei) collide to form a nucleus of beryllium-8, which in turn is hit by a third alpha particle before it has time to break up. Fred Hoyle and Willie Fowler worked on the analysis of this process for some time; they suspected that this was how heavy nuclei might be built up inside stars. They saw the possibility that the energy levels of beryllium, helium, and carbon might form the right combination to carry out Salpeter's idea. Hoyle's concept turned out to be correct. He showed that all that was required to ensure success was for the phenomenon of "resonance" to take place, which, in simple terms, is a dynamic means of matching energies of particles to encourage them to combine.

Hoyle calculated that the temperature required for the process was contained within stars and was just right to meet such conditions. He was the first scientist to prove that all heavy elements were, in fact, built up in the core of stars. It was one of Hoyle's most brilliant achievements.

When ordinary stars die, the elements that they built up remain and the star reduces to a white dwarf of enormous density, giving rise to black holes. When giant stars die, they explode, as stated earlier, and scatter their contents into space. Atoms from these elements eventually form each one of us. Each carbon atom in our body can be traced back to stars that exploded long before our solar system had formed. Gribbin and Rees put it well when they said: "Without supernovae we would not be here. So the rules of physics that allow supernovae to exist also allow us to exist."

Quasars, discovered in 1971 by Australian astronomers, have independently placed limits on the size of the universe. These quasars (quasi-stars or strange stars) appear very like tiny stars on a photographic plate. But when their light was analysed it was clear that they were thousands of millions of light-years away—far outside our Milky Way galaxy. They were emitting very large amounts of radiation, and it was thought that these quasars were galaxies in the making. The theory is that they get their energy from supermassive black holes at their cores. The process has been compared to a cosmic drain plug shredding stars and sucking in gas that spirals down the drain plug while developing enormous temperatures. This gives rise to vast amounts of radiation, which we can detect on Earth. Quasars are no different from other galaxies in formation except that they started much later in cosmic time. They decrease in number as they reach or exceed 18 billion light-years from us. Their distance has been measured by carefully relating the red shift of their light with their velocity of recession. So quasars tell us still more about the early history of the universe; while the telescope can

be compared to a time machine: when one look one is really looking back into time. Light from travelling for 18,000 million years—four time life of our solar system.

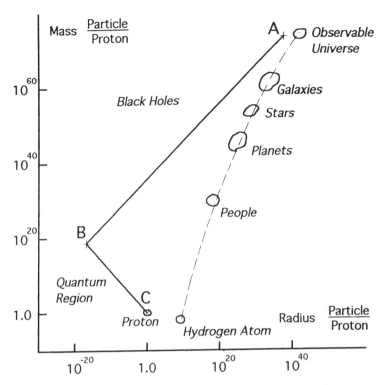

Figure 16. Characteristic masses and radii of various objects from atoms to entire universe (plotted to log scale) (after Gribbin and Rees).

The area at the top left-hand side corresponds to plots of black holes (objects of enormous density and mass resulting from collapse of stars). The region on the other side of AB corresponds to plots of galaxies, planets, people, and atoms. Again the plots lie almost on a straight line. There is then the region to the left of BC, which corresponds to objects that are extremely small and almost devoid of mass. Quantum mechanics tells us that such objects have no "real" existence. There is uncertainty as to the location of such particles, but the concept of size becomes diffuse.

127

It is evident that the range of size of all known objects lies within a comparatively narrow band extending from a proton (point C) to a galaxy (point A).

There are other laws and orders that govern aspects of the world about us independent of the laws known to us. They manifest themselves as regularities or irregularities, such as the precision of the solar system; turbulent and streamline flows in fluids; vagaries in climatic conditions; ability of organisms to heal themselves; capacity of animal and plant cells to replicate themselves having regard for the billions that do so; the forces that accurately guide migratory birds over thousands of miles to reach their intended destinations without previously having been there; and the forces that direct certain species of fish to return to their place of birth from distant seas.

There are many examples of such laws together with the role they play in the self-creating, self-organising world. None have a scientific explanation known to us; all are associated with numerous scientific theories and opinions. Some of these theories are ingenious; none is fact.

The origin of these indefinable laws must have been subsequent to the big bang, after which they unfolded themselves in a unidirectional fashion, symbolising the ''arrow of time,'' which always points forward.

If the Newtonian theory (of a clockwork world) or the thermodynamic theory (claiming that everything started in an orderly way) were correct, the universal laws and constants of nature would have no place. But they have a very real place. The above two theories are not accurate. The Newtonian theory is approximately correct—but not at all good enough for high-energy particles. The thermodynamic theory, on the other hand, is statistical. While the world may be sliding into a featureless pit, it is also growing, creating, and developing since its origin.

The universe is indeterministic; it is intrinsically unpredictable. It has a freedom of choice; it is in no way conventional; it accelerates using its powers of creativity. No two people are alike; no two blades of grass are alike. The human condition endeavours to have us all alike, dress alike, live alike, one imitating the other ad nauseam, and contented to do so. But the world is not like that: everything is so different with the certainty of indeterminism. If the laws and physical constants differed from those that existed for billions of years, for example, the universe would have altered radically: the solar system would be vastly different and carbon-based life, as we know it, would have been very different, or nonexistent.

Let us contemplate just a few of the laws that maintain our equilibrium:

1. One of the many reasons the model of the big bang is considered a scientific triumph is because it explains the abundance of the lightest elements; hydrogen, 75 percent of the universe, and helium, 25 percent. Spectroscopic studies of gas clouds and old stars confirm these values. The standard model of the universe also explains how these elements were made from primordial baryons (protons and neutrons). It does not matter how the universe generated the enormous heat and density that it did in the first instance; what does matter is that it was subjected to enormous temperature and pressure. This established a clean sweep and obliterated the past, if indeed such existed.

2. If the force of gravity operated on an inverse cube law instead of an inverse square law, then planetary orbits would be quite unstable and a planet that should dare move a little closer to the sun would immediately fall into the sun while that which should happen to move a little farther away in its orbit would continue to do so.

3. It was Einstein who spotted the fact that the dimensionality in the law of gravity is always one less than the

dimensionality of space. This is the law of inverse square, in space of three dimensions, and an inverse cube in space of four dimensions. Thus the orbits of planets are stable only in a space of three dimensions.

4. We have seen that all stars begin their lives by burning hydrogen, converting the results to helium, and releasing enormous amounts of heat energy in doing so. When helium is burned it produces carbon. This is the stage in the life of a star when it swells up to become a red giant. We saw that in the case of the very large stars (there is a critical size) many times the mass of the sun, they end their lives by exploding and scattering their contents. This is the source of the elements, as mentioned earlier. Were stars made for us or us for the stars?

5. The step-by-step process by which the various elements (hydrogen, helium, carbon, oxygen, nitrogen, phosphorus, etc.) are *BUILT* up, one from the other, is more than a cosmic coincidence when the celestial laboratories (stars) in which they are built are themselves taken into account.

6. The law that enables us to measure distance and velocity of recession of stars or galaxies is based on characteristics of atomic structure. Measurements may be obtained even though the objects in question are thousands of light-years away. A refinement of the Döppler effect for light is used. But we should not let its ingenuity go unnoticed; there is a beauty in the symmetry of this very phenomenon: just as electrons can occupy different energy levels, like steps on a staircase, so too can the particles that make up the nucleus of an atom. Protons and neutrons can change from a low-energy state to a high-energy state if they are given a push (a specific amount of energy). They may fall

back to a lower level later, even to the bottom step of the stairs, should they give back or radiate the appropriate energy. The amount of energy involved depends on the size of each step and the number of steps the electron jumped in one hop. Atoms thus absorb energy from background light, which leaves a "fingerprint" in the spectrum. These "fingerprints" can be studied in the laboratory and their wavelength predicted using quantum theory. The success of quantum theory in explaining the spectrum of hydrogen was one of the great triumphs of physics in the twentieth century. In short, we have an accurate method of measuring distance to remote stars, galaxies, and quasars.

7. The special theory of relativity is based on two postulates: (a) the laws of physics may be expressed in equations having the same form in all frames of reference moving at constant velocity with respect to one another; and (b) the velocity of light in free space has the same value for all observers, regardless of their state of motion. From these emerge a new mechanics in which there is an intimate relationship between space and time, mass and energy. Without these relationships it would be impossible to understand the microscopic world within the atom—the basis of modern physics. So the velocity of light, in every direction, is the unifying factor relating mass, energy, and time. What a cosmic mess we would find ourselves in if special relativity was not accurate and correct.

8. That physical constants go to building atomic nuclei to be in tune with the organic or inorganic environment is more of a coincidence than the processes referred to in 5 above. It is clear that there is a never-ending creativity built into the universe. For example, a complicated biological organism must evolve in step with its

environment to survive. The physical laws governing the genetic code of a particular organism are set; there is no going back to modify them. Again, ordinary matter, which is composed of protons, neutrons, and electrons, would seem adequate to account for the structures of the universe around us. But not all nuclei are stable, and additional fundamental particles known as neutrinos are necessary to accelerate beta decay and hence a more appropriate configuration. (See figure 14.)

9. Water, as distinct from other liquids, has an unusual feature with respect to life. When it is heated it contracts between 0°C and 4°C and expands from 4°C to 100°C. Its maximum density occurs at 4°C. In Arctic regions, water immediately below the ice is at 0°C, but it is 4°C at the bottom, thus allowing marine and plant life on Earth always to survive in severe winters at the bottom of a frozen lake. We are back to the intriguing question: Were the unusual characteristics of water designed to suit animal and plant life, or was it the other way around? Whichever way it was, it has played a key role in the evolution of life on Earth.

10. The large-scale structure and motion of the universe are remarkable. Yet gravity operates to restrain expansion and cause it to slow down. The universe is the product of a competition between the explosive power of the big bang and the forces of gravity pulling all the pieces back together. Recently astrophysicists have come to realise just how delicately balanced this competition is. As stated earlier, had the big bang been weaker, the cosmos would soon have fallen back into a big crunch. Had it been stronger, the cosmic material would have dispersed so rapidly that galaxies would not have formed. The structure of the universe, then, is dependent on a sensitive balance and matching of explosive

power and gravitational power. Modern thinking has come to the conclusion that this matching is extremely delicate; it is believed by some, as we have said, that the matching is accurate to an extraordinary degree of one part in 10^{60}.

11. There is also the mystery of why the universe is so uniform in distribution of matter and rate of expansion. Explosions are usually chaotic affairs, and one might expect the big bang to have varied in its degree of activity from place to place. But this is not so.

There is a law underlying these coincidences that ensures that "life goes on"; it also ensures that natural processes and constants keep in step. To quote Ilya Prigogine: "God is no more an archivist unfolding an infinite sequence he had designed once and forever. He continues the labour of creation throughout time." Freeman Dyson said: "In some sense the universe knew we were coming." Sir Fred Hoyle, on the same topic, in *Galaxies, Nuclei and Quasars* wrote: "The laws of physics have been deliberately designed with regard to the consequences they produce inside stars. We exist only in portions of the universe where the energy levels in carbon and oxygen nuclei happen to be correctly placed."

Are physical systems, like those enumerated, holistic? Do they possess laws that cannot be reduced to the laws of elementary forces and particles? To date no holistic laws of physics have been found. Such concepts as temperature and pressure are meaningless at the molecular level. When we can understand telepathy, for example, and discover the holistic laws that govern that phenomenon, another contribution to science will have occurred. To date, physics makes its limited contribution through reductionism. Holistic aspects are more appropriate to the science of perception, even though quantum theory and the physics of self-organising are holistic in concept.

If the universe is full of symmetry it is also violent; when we think we are comprehending certain aspects, we get a mental jolt when we come up against matters quite the contrary to what we thought we understood.

Yes, it is claimed that the universe is simple, but it is also sprinkled with violent activity: explosions of stars, disturbances in galaxies, collisions of celestial bodies. Have these events a purpose? Are we obliged to regard them as inexplicable laws and constants of nature with a technological character until we find otherwise? They appear to be tuned to a degree that contains an enormous information content. Is it inescapable that it plays a universal role? Since we don't know what the role is, we substitute the term *God,* who, it is assumed, is an omnipotent Being with infinite comprehension and mind, whereas the mind of man is finite.

Chapter 20
Belief

It is fashionable with some scientists when discussing the origin of matter or the origin of the universe to indulge in the ''scientific method.'' This simply embraces procedures such as experiment, deductive reasoning, observation, hypothesis, assumption, and even mathematical methods. All of them are based on reasonable ''arguments which are functions of mental processes'' derived from sensory experience.

Humans have always had belief in a higher order. Belief has ranged from reasoned argument to blind faith. If quantum effects in brain cells are taken into account (the indeterministic aspect of thought), it is probable that reasoned argument will not suffice. It is in this field that clergy of every denomination, institution, and creed flourish; simple faith has always survived in spite of these gentlemen. Faith is as old as time; it is also a mysterious component of brain functions.

We have seen that science has very few answers to a host of natural phenomenon. The scientific method draws many blanks, no matter how carefully one is committed. Notwithstanding, many authors of works relating to natural laws, cosmology, or biology go to extraordinary lengths to explain away the origin of things. For some reason, never clearly explained, they avoid the possibility that the origin, or behaviour, of natural phenomenon may lie with a Superior Being or Intelligence Content or A hidden hand.

Debate concerning the origin of the universe presupposes that it had an origin. Ancient cultures, however, believed that it did not have a specific beginning but consisted of endless cycles of creation. Primitive cultures base their concept on the cycle of the seasons. They had no other interest in the origin or fate of the universe. Their faith relied largely on myth or superstition to carry them through; faith was present.

The early civilisations of China differed little from such concepts except in respect to the length of the cycles. Each cycle began with a new dynasty and ended with its fall. The Hindu culture relied on a similar system, except that the cycle of renewal of creation was very much longer. The ancient Greeks believed likewise until the coming of Plato and Aristotle, who asserted that the universe must have a cause and that cause was God. Such thinking was expanded by Saint Augustine and to a lesser extent by Saint Thomas Aquinas. The concept became known as the cosmological argument for the existence of God. It took two forms: causal argument and the argument from contingency. Many, including David Hume and Immanuel Kant, treated this approach with scepticism; Bertrand Russell treated it with contempt.

Causal argument proceeded as follows: Every event requires a cause. There cannot be an infinite chain of causes, so there must have been a first cause for everything. This cause is God. Many interpretations of the argument exist; they all tend to avoid simplicity at the expense of quality thinking. The most serious objection to the causal argument was the fact that cause and effect are functions of time—the target shatters when the bullet is fired. In this sense it is meaningless to talk about God creating the universe in a causal sense if the act of creation involves the creation of time itself. If there was no ''before'' there can be no cause.

The contingent argument is based on the concept that an explanation for the features of the universe depends on something other than its existence—something beyond itself. While it is easy to imagine something else, there is no guarantee that the "something else" is possible or viable. Are the laws of physics violated in such an eventuality? The laws of physics that we know of are surprisingly well integrated.

It is the causal argument, however, that occupied the minds of philosophers, churchmen, and scientists in very early times. Saint Augustine of Hippo (354–430) was the first to recognise that time was part of the physical universe (part of creation). He placed the Creator firmly outside time. He ridiculed the idea of God waiting for an infinite time and then deciding, at some appropriate moment, to create the universe. Augustine wrote: "The world and time had both one beginning. The world was made not in time, but simultaneously with time."

Saint Thomas Aquinas (1225–74) developed the legacy of ancient thought. He combined Christian thought with Greek methods of rational philosophy. He had difficulty in relating well-defined qualities of God (perfection, simplicity, timelessness, omnipotence) to a time-dependent physical universe. It is inevitable, therefore, that a variety of theological doctrines prevail.

Deism, belief in a divine being who set off the universe, let it roll, and watched events unfold from afar without interfering.

Theism, belief in God, Creator of the universe, who remains directly involved in the day-to-day running of it and of human beings with whom He retains a personal relationship.

Pantheism, belief that God is identified with nature itself. Everything is part of God, and God is everything.

As Paul Davies states, "There are many scientists who are critical of organised religion not because of their personal spiritual content, but for their perverting influence on otherwise decent

137

human behaviour, especially when they involve themselves in power politics.'' The physicist Hermann Bondi was a harsh critic of religion, which he regarded as a ''serious and habit-forming evil.''

It is clear that a huge variety of beliefs must prevail depending on the individual, his emotional content, and his background. It seems to me that one stands alone on his own two feet in this world with respect to conscience, belief, and faith.

There is a agreement amongst the distinguished scientists that the universe began with a singularity or big bang. The concept makes it difficult for philosophers and scientists to relate the big bang to time, God, and what went before time.

It was Albert Einstein, who showed in his general theory of relativity in 1915, that matter cannot be separated from space and time. The concept took fellow scientists a number of years to verify and accept. It is now accepted. Saint Augustine was surprisingly accurate in his time!

It is often said in relation to origin and expansion of the universe that if one could imagine running the cosmic movie backwards, then the galaxies would come back together and merge. This would result in the galactic material becoming compressed to enormous densities, leading to a big bang. But this took place approximately 20 billion years ago. Is there some similarity, however poetic, between this concept and the contents of the first book of Genesis?

Prior to Einstein's work, theological doctrines in relation to ''God,'' ''infinity,'' and ''matter'' were numerous. Previously, people asked, ''Where did the big bang occur?'' The big bang did not occur at a point in space. Space itself came into existence with the big bang. There was the same difficulty in regard to the question: What happened before the big bang? Saint Augustine proclaimed in the fifth century that ''the universe was made with time and not in time.'' His statement corresponds exactly with the modern scientific view, which is based on Einstein's space/

time warp. Scientists did have difficulty in accepting this and proceeded to construct their own theories and attempt to avoid the singularity or big bang. But now the majority accept Einstein's findings as profound truths. Dr. Kit Pedlar, who represents a large body of pathologists and scientists, said recently:

> For almost twenty years I occupied my research time as a happy biological reductionist believing that my painstaking research would eventually reveal ultimate truths. Then I began to read the new physics. The experience was shattering.
>
> As a biologist I had imagined the physicists to be cool, clear, unemotional men and women who looked down on nature from a clinical detached viewpoint—people who reduced a sunset to wavelengths and frequencies, and observers who shredded the complex of the universe into rigid and formal elements.
>
> My error was enormous. I began to study the works of people with legendary names: Einstein, Böhr, Schrödinger and Dirac. I found that here were not clinical and detached men, but poetic and religious ones who imagined such unfamiliar immensities as to make what I have referred to as the "paranormal" almost pedestrian by comparison.

It might well be said that for most of us to make any sense of the universal world about us, a poetic approach, tinged with a vivid imagination and lively faith, would enable us to wander through the cosmos with amazement and delight.

In one of his infrequent outbursts Niels Bohr claimed, "Anyone who is not shocked by quantum theory has not understood it."

Gustav Jung, writing on "the extraordinary beauty of the human mind" said: "I simply believe that some part of the human self or soul is not subject to the laws of space and time."

On the other hand, Fred Hoyle said: "I have always thought it curious that, while most scientists claim to eschew religion, it actually dominates their thoughts more than it does the clergy."

Throughout the history of science there has been an abundance of hard-nosed scientists whose perspective of their observations was one thing, but there has also been an equal number of soft-nosed scientists whose perspective was different. It is not that one group was correct and the other was not; it is that there is an equal place for both.

Appendices

Appendix 1
Relativity Coefficient

The special theory of relativity that forms the basis for both the general theory of relativity and the laws of geometrodynamics rests on the fact that the speed of light in a vacuum is constant at 670 million miles per hour irrespective of the speed of its source. Mathematical logic therefore dictates that the length of a moving spacecraft in the direction of motion must be reduced in proportion to its speed. Likewise the spacecraft mass, that is, the energy required to accelerate it, is increased as the object accelerates. All "clocks" aboard the spacecraft (including astronauts wristwatches and the aging process of their bodies) slow down as the spacecraft accelerates.

The extent of these changes is calculated by three simple formulae:

1. The *length* of a moving spacecraft must be multiplied by the expression

$$\sqrt{\left(1 - \frac{v^2}{c^2}\right)}$$

when v is speed of spacecraft and c is speed of light.

2. The increased *mass* of moving spacecraft is obtained by multiplying its rest mass by the expression:

$$\sqrt{\left(1-\frac{v^2}{c^2}\right)}$$

3. Measuring the slowing of *time* on board the spacecraft is equally simple. To see how much more slowly the astronauts are aging, we multiply a given period, say sixty minutes of Earth time, by the expression

$$\sqrt{\left(1-\frac{v^2}{c^2}\right)}$$

One of the most surprising features of these characteristics is that two spacecraft cannot recede from one another at a combined speed which is greater than the speed of light. Take an extreme example: suppose a man sees two beams of light receding in opposite directions. He will estimate their mutual speed of recession as twice that of light or 2c. But if he were riding on one of those beams, he would estimate the other's speed of recession, according to the formula as

$$\frac{c + c}{1 + \frac{c^2}{c^2}}$$

Which works out as c.

Table C

Speed of craft as percentage of light	Length of craft(meters)	Mass (tonnes)	Duration of a craft-hour in minutes (Earth = 60)
0	100.00	100.00	60.00
20	97.98	102.10	58.70
40	91.65	109.11	55.00
60	80.00	125.00	48.00
80	60.00	166.67	36.00
90	49.59	229.42	26.18
95	31.22	320.26	18.71
99	14.11	708.88	8.53
99.9	4.47	2236.63	2.78
99.997	0.71	14,142.20	1.17
100	zero	infinity	zero

From the values in Table C above it is evident that no craft can travel at the speed of light, since it would have developed infinite mass, requiring infinite power to drive it.

While these values can form with the test results known to date, using particle accelerators, it does not mean that, one day—be it a hundred years hence a breakthrough in our knowledge may occur which will show how matter can be got to move faster than light.

Appendix 2
The Four Fundamental Forces (Table A)

Table A. The Four Fundamental Forces

INTERACTION	PARTICLES AFFECTED	RANGE	RELATIVE STRENGTH	PARTICLES EXCHANGED
Strong nuclear force	Hadrons	$\sim10^{-15}$m	1	Mesons
Electromagnetic force	Charged particles	00	$\sim10^{-2}$	Photons
Weak force	Hadrons and leptons	$\sim10^{-17}$m	$\sim10^{-13}$	Intermediate bosons
Gravitational force	All	00	$\sim10^{-40}$	Gravitons

Appendix 3
Inverse Square Law

Two charges, or forces, of magnitude q_1 and q_2 situated a distance d apart will attract or repel each other with a force F where

F is proportional to $\dfrac{q_1 \, q_2}{d^2}$

Therefore $F = \dfrac{\lambda \, q_1 \, q_2}{d^2}$

where λ is a constant whose value depends upon the units in which q, d, and F are measured. By a suitable choice of units, we can make $\lambda = 1$. This is the law of inverse squares.

Appendix 4
Quantum Effects

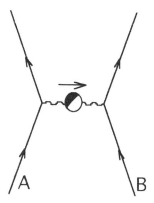

Figure 4. Quantum effects are important. Energy can be transmitted in discrete lumps. For example, photons of light are quanta of electromagnetic field, so when two electric particles, A and B, approach each other, they are influenced by their mutual electromagnetic fields, and forces are generated between them that cause the particles A and B to deviate. This figure shows a single photon being transferred between two electrons. Think of two tennis players whose play is coupled via the exchange of the tennis ball. Photons act in a way rather similar to the tennis ball and keep the electrons in communication. It is a subtle and important phenomenon. Inside the nucleus, pions (another fundamental particle) flit back and forth between neutrons and protons, glueing them together with nuclear force.

It is the behaviour of fundamental particles such as pions, quarks, etc., within the atom that is unique in this universe, yet it is their behaviour that ensures the very stability of matter!

Appendix 5
Protein Molecule

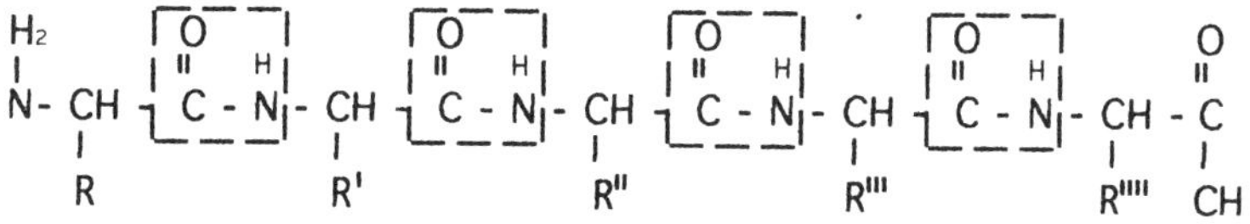

Figure 6. Basic structure of a protein molecule—a peptide linkage of amino acids.

A protein has two essential elements in its structure: a carboxyl group (NH₂) and an amino group (COOH).

Appendix 6
Energy-Rich Compound

ATP is a substance found universally in living cells. It is an "energy-rich" compound that by transferring its terminal phosphate group to another molecule such as glucose can convert a relatively inert substance into a reactive one. ATP is the immediate source of energy for the many synthetic and other reactions needed for the maintenance of life.

Muscular contraction in animals, depends on the free energy librated by hydrolysis (that is the decomposition of a compound by reaction with water) of ATP. While much of its mode of action is obscure, nevertheless, it is possible to form an idea of what goes on: the contraction of a muscle fibre is actuated by structures in the cell called myofibrils, which run parallel to the axis of the fibre. In cross-section a myofibril presents roughly the appearance shown below. (See Figure 17.)

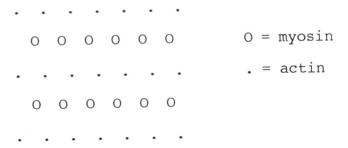

Figure 17. Myofibril in Muscle

Contraction of the myofibril is due to actin and myson threads sliding relatively to one another due to the energy transfer provided by ATP.

Appendix 7
Elementary Particles (Table B)

CLASS	NAME	PARTICLE	ANTI-PARTICLE	REST MASS, MeV	MEAN LIFE, (seconds)
MASSLESS BOSON	Photon	γ	(γ)	0	Stable
LEPTON	e-neutrino	ν_e	$\bar{\nu}_e$	0	Stable
	μ-neutrino	ν_μ	$\bar{\nu}_\mu$	0	Stable
	Electron	e^-	e^+	0.51	Stable
	Muon	μ^-	μ^+	106	2.2×10^{-6}
MESON	Pion	π^+	π^-	140	2.6×10^{-8}
		π^0	(π^0)	135	8×10^{-17}
		π^-	π^+	140	2.6×10^{-8}
	Kaon	K^+	K^-	494	1.2×10^{-18}
		K^0	$\bar{K}^0$	498	9×10^{-11} / 5×10^{-8}
	η meson	η^0	(η^0)	549	2.5×10^{-19}
BARYON	Nucleon { Proton	$\bar{p}$	$\bar{p}$	938.3	Stable
	Nucleon { Neutron	$\bar{n}$	$\bar{n}$	939.6	932
	Λ hyperon	Λo	Λo	1,116	2.5×10^{-10}
	Σ hyperon	$\bar{\Sigma}+$	$\bar{\Sigma}-$	1,189	8.0×10^{-11}
		$\bar{\Sigma}o$	$\bar{\Sigma}o$	1,192	10^{-14}
		$\bar{\Sigma}-$	$\bar{\Sigma}+$	1,197	1.5×10^{-10}
	Ξ hyperon	Ξ^0	Ξ^0	1,315	3.0×10^{-10}
		Ξ^-	Ξ^+	1,321	1.7×10^{-10}
	Ω^- hyperon	Ω^-	Ω^+	1,672	1.3×10^{-10}

Table B. Elementary particles stable against decay by the strong interaction. Mesons and Baryons are jointly considered Hadrons and are believed to be composed of quarks.

BIBLIOGRAPHY

Augustine of Hippo. Translated by M. Dos. *The City of God* (Riverside, N.J.: Hafner, 1948)

Augustine of Hippo. *Confessions, Book 12* (N.P.: Loeb Classical Library, n.d.), Ch. 7

Aquinas, Thomas. *Summa Theologica.* Edited by T. Gilby (N.P.: Eyre and Spottiswood, 1964)

Böhr, Niels. *Atomic Theory and the Description of Nature* (Cambridge: Cambridge University Press, 1934)

Calder, Nigel. *The Key to the Universe* (New York: Viking Press, 1977)

Calder, Nigel. *Einstein's Universe* (London: BBC Publication, 1979)

Crick, Francis. *Life Itself, Its Origin and Nature* (New York: Simon & Schuster, 1982)

Darwin, Charles. *Origins of the Species* (London: N. P. 1859)

Dawkins, Richard. *The Blind Watchmaker* (New York and London: Penguin and Norton, 1987)

de Broglie, L. Nobel Prize Address (N.P.: Boorse and Motz, 1929)

d'Espaynat, Bernard. *Quantum Theory and Reality* (Berkshire: Benjamin, 1971)

Davies, Paul. *God and the New Physics* (London: Dent, 1983)

Davies, Paul. *The Cosmic Blueprint* (New York: Simon & Schuster, 1989)

Einstein, Albert. *The Meaning of Relativity* (London: Methuen, 1922)

Gamon, George. *A Star Called the Sun* (Harmondsworth, Middlesex: Penguin, 1964)

Gamon, George. *The Creation of the Universe* (New York: Viking Press, 1952)

Glashow, Sheldon. "Quarks with Colour and Flavour," *Scientific American*, 1975

Gribbin, John. *In Search of the Big Bang* (London: Heineman, 1986)

Gribbin, J. and Rees, M. *Cosmic Coincidences* (New York and London: Bantam Press, 1989)

Gribbin, J. and Rees, M. *The Stuff of the Universe* (London: Heineman, 1990)

Heisenberg, Werner. *Physics and Beyond* (London: Allen and Unwin, 1971)

Hoyle, Sir Fred. *The Intelligent Universe* (London: Michael Joseph, 1983)

Hoyle, Fred and Wicramasingle, Chandra. *Evolution from Space* (London: Dent, 1981), 2d Ed.

Hoffman, Banesh. *The Strange Story of the Quantum* (New York: Dover, 1959)

Hawkins, Stephen. *A Brief History of Time* (New York and London: Bantam, 1988)

Jeans, Sir James. *The Universe Around Us* (Cambridge: Cambridge University Press, 1930)

MacKay, Donald M. *The Clockwork Image* (London: Inter Varsity Press, 1974)

Newton, Sir Isaac. *Philosoiphiae Naturalis Principia Mathematica Bk III.* General Scholium, 1687

Peacock, Arthur. *The Sciences and Theology in the Twentieth Century* (Stockfield: Oriel, 1981)

Prigogine, Ilya and Stengers, Isabella. *Order out of Chaos* (London: Heineman, 1984)

Pascal, Blaise. *Pensees sur la Religion* (Paris: N.P. 1676)

Rose, Stephen. *Making of Memory: from Molecules to Mind* (London: Bantam, 1992)

Schilpp, Arthur. *Albert Einstein: Philosopher Scientist* (Cambridge: Cambridge University Press, 1952)

Shkovskii, I. S. and Sagan, Carl. *Intelligent Life in the Universe* (N.P.: Holden Day Merryfield, 1966)

Stannard, Russell. *Grounds for Reasonable Belief* (Edinburgh: Scottish Academy Press, 1989)

Sheldrake, Rupert. *A New Science of Life* (London: Blond and Briggs, 1981)

Weinberg, Steven. *The First Three Minutes* (London: Andre Deutch, 1977)